Magnolia Avenue

Magnolia Avenue

JOSEPH R. JONES

Deeds Publishing | Athens

Published by Deeds Publishing in Athens, GA
www.deedspublishing.com

Printed in The United States of America

Cover design by Mark Babcock.

ISBN 978-1-950794-28-7

Books are available in quantity for promotional or premium use. For information, email info@deedspublishing.com.

First Edition, 2020

10 9 8 7 6 5 4 3 2 1

Characters

JACKSON	An English professor on sabbatical
PHOEBE	Jackson's neighbor
CORBIN	Auden and Victoria's nephew
MS. SALLY	Jackson's childhood nanny
SARAH BETH	Jackson's older sister
BOYCE	An older neighbor on Magnolia Avenue
JOSHUA	Sarah Beth's son
AUBREY	Lives on First Avenue in the District
VICTORIA	A federal judge who is married to Auden
WHIT	An eccentric neighbor
CARA	Boyce's next door neighbor
AUDEN	Prominent attorney married to Victoria
ELIZABETH HATHAWAY	Auden and Victoria's neighbor
PATRICK HATHAWAY	Physician married to Elizabeth Hathaway
ERIC	Owns a chain of convenience stores
EMILY	Married to Eric
BLAKE	Jackson and Sarah Beth's brother
ABBY	Charleston native and in Culpepper for work

Jackson

I TURNED MY WRANGLER LEFT ONTO THE RED BRICK
streets of Magnolia Avenue. As the tires met the red bricks,
Faulkner, my white Labrador retriever, sat up immediately and
glanced out the window. The noise of the rubber on the dried
baked clay awakened him from his snoring. We passed a large
sign that read "Welcome to Culpepper's Historic District." The
homes were magnanimous and stoic. The homes, all southern in
nature, were divided by two red brick lanes that went in opposite
directions. A large median separated the brick streets; the median was the home to hundreds of mature magnolia trees. It was
obvious the trees had been there for decades. I drove slowly. The
memories of my childhood rose into the air with each thump of
the tires meeting the hard clay.

I approached my childhood home, a house surrounded with
huge columns and several rocking chairs and porch swings. The
State of Mississippi flag floated in the wind. I stopped in front
of our old home, and peered into my past. The memories inundated my mind. As a child, I would jump off the front porch
pretending to be Spiderman and run over to the tire swing that

hung from an old oak tree in the side yard. The innocence of my childhood hid the reality of the true darkness that existed in that house. As I aged, the innocence was ripped from my soul. I hated my father. I hated what he did to me, to Ms. Sally, to my little brother. I hated that he died gracefully in that house. He didn't deserve grace. He didn't deserve dignity. I stood there staring at the reality of a past that I wished I could forget. The smell of the river permeated my nostrils, which jolted me to reality.

After my parents died, the home has remained empty.

I pressed the pedal and continued slowly down the street. Faulkner held his head outside the vehicle fighting with the wind. The homes were the same as they were when I was a child, most, even the same the color. The historic preservation board rarely approved any changes to the outward appearance of the buildings. The further I drove, the sizes of the houses diminished, not too dramatically, but it was noticeable.

When I travelled four blocks of the total seven blocks of the historic district, I turned right into the driveway. The house was a large antebellum structure built in the early 1900s. Six white columns that extended the full height of the structure. The columns were the focal point of the front of the home. An Ole Miss Football flag waved vicariously in the wind. There were four wooden rocking chairs placed perfectly across the porch. Four ceiling fans circulated the hot June air. Uncle Bronwyn Kensington had lived in the house most of his adult life. He was my father's brother. He was a rigid and handsome bachelor who never married. He inherited this home from his parents, as did my father inherit our home from Big Daddy.

I parked the Jeep, and Faulkner and I climbed out. We walked onto the porch. I entered the key and turned the door knob slightly to the right. The smell of avoidance pervaded my nostrils.

The chaos of my childhood meandered slowly through my mind. The fear and the anger from growing up in the historic district of Culpepper, Mississippi surfaced in my thoughts. He was dead. It was different now. I hoped it would be different this time.

Uncle Bronwyn bequeathed his house to me a few years ago when he passed; yet, this was the first time I had entered the structure in five years. After his death, I hired Ms. Sally and Mr. Jim to care for the house, as they did my family home. Ms. Sally cleaned the house twice a month, and Mr. Jim handled any outdoor maintenance that was required.

As an English professor at Stuart College in Virginia, I was offered a sabbatical to write my new novel. I walked back to the front porch. I stood there staring into the equanimity of the sunrise.

After I stood there for a few moments, I heard Faulkner bark and felt his fur rub the outside of my right leg as he ran past me across the brick street into the median. I ran after him screaming. He finally stopped and sat perfectly still in front of an older white man. The man slowly walked over to Faulkner and brushed his hand on Faulkner's face. Faulkner was completely calm and received the old man's affection. When I reached Faulkner, I apologized. The old man acknowledged my comments with a slight nod. The smell of alcohol radiated from his pores. He stood, waved goodbye to Faulkner, and reached his hand out toward me. I reached for it. As he grasped my hand to shake it, I noticed callouses that covered the inside of his hand. The rough patches of skin were abrasive to my own palms. His eyes met mine. Without a word, he released my hand and walked away. I watched as he crossed the other side of the red bricks walking toward First Avenue.

I scolded Faulkner, and pointed toward Uncle Bronwyn's house.

Phoebe

I STEPPED OUT OF THE SHOWER, AND NOTICED HIM lying in my bed. The street light from the window illuminated his body. He motioned for me to come to him. He stood, and his hands gracefully held me. His breath was soft and comforting as it rolled over my neck.

Corbin was in his mid-twenties. He worked for Auden Harrington, his uncle. Auden lived on the north end of Magnolia with his wife, Victoria.

Corbin and I have been casually dating for a few months, though Corbin wants it to remain publicly reticent. I had given him the code to enter my house a few weeks ago, so I have become accustomed to his early arrivals. He was young, but there was something that drew me to him.

He slipped out the side door through the side gate which opened onto Magnolia.

Corbin was a place holder. A place holder for what I was unsure. But, he was needed. My husband was killed several years ago. He was a police officer in Jackson. For years, he was an officer in Culpepper, but JPD offered him more money and a better schedule. Sam was stunningly handsome, and he was the perfect husband. We raised one girl together, who lives at Fort Jones with her husband, an army officer. Sam went to work, and a gunman ran into the police station. With an AR-15, he killed ten officers before he was shot. Sam was one of the ten. He died alone on the floor in the chaos. No one was there holding his hand. I know that I will never remarry because he was my soul mate. He completed me in ways that no one else can. It has been seven years, but I still miss him.

As I walked through the front door to retrieve the morning paper, a man standing on Old Man Bronwyn's front porch caught my attention. I waved, and he returned the gesture.

The air was cooler, and the smell of fish from the river was more apparent this morning. The river, which ran parallel to Magnolia, was one block behind our houses. Often the smell of fish was common during the early spring and summer months, but this morning it seemed to be overbearing.

I reached and clutched the paper. I walked slowly into my house glancing at the man standing on the porch.

Old Man Bronwyn was a character. I knew him for a few years before he died. His family was one of the old Culpepper families who founded the town. I think his family owned one of the mills on Fourth Avenue many years ago. He was a unique man who never married. His brother lived in the large home at the other end of Magnolia. I am not sure how close they were because I rarely saw them together. I rarely saw Bronwyn with anyone, and I rarely saw anyone at his home.

The man on the porch worried me. No one but Ms. Sally and Mr. Jim has been at that house in years. Did he buy the house? Was he just standing on the porch? Who was he? I will call Victoria. Maybe she would know. If not, I will call the police.

I closed the door, but the smell of fish floated through before I did.

Corbin

THE COLD AIR SLAPPED MY RED FACE AS I WALKED out of her side gate. My heart was still racing. Normally, I am not into older women, but sex with her has been great the last few times. Not as good as Cara or Aubrey, but a close runner-up.

Sex was about the adrenaline rush. I kept a list of all of the people with whom I have had sex and the dates. This morning Phoebe moved me into the four digits, which made me smile. It wasn't about the act; it was about the number and the ability to do it emotionlessly. It was also about the ability to keep it all hidden from everyone else.

I am going to be late for work, and my uncle is going to kill me. Uncle Auden was a man who abided by principles and believed that a man's word and a handshake were the only assurances he needed. He was an amazing attorney, one of the most successful attorneys in the state. He had even helped me one time. He and Victoria had built a wonderful life here. I was glad they believed in me.

I walked north on Magnolia, I noticed a man standing on Phoebe's neighbor's front porch.

"Good morning," I said.

"Good morning," he replied.

I continued my journey to work. I have never seen him around the neighborhood. He was tall with short blonde hair. His eyes fixated on the sun-rise. A white lab lay on the porch beside his feet. A black Jeep Wrangler rested in the driveway with Virginia plates.

Jackson

AS THE SUN ROSE, I WALKED UP THE SIDEWALK TO the commercial part of Magnolia for breakfast. From my uncle's home, it was only a nine block walk. As I ate, I watched people meander through their morning lives. Afterward, I walked over to First Baptist Church, which was nestled among other churches on Second Avenue. It has been years since I was there, yet the structure remained the same over the years. Deep red clay bricks created the entire outside of the massive structure. There were six monstrous deep beige columns across the front of the building. The columns seemed just as large to me as an adult as they did when I ran around them as a child. The large bowl shaped fountain that my mother commissioned for the church still remained on the right side of the main entrance, spraying water into the air. It was a beautiful remembrance of my mother's dedication to her faith. There were planters on the front that contained ferns. The lawn was meticulously manicured. The slight morning breeze birthed a clanking from the chain on the flag pole that held the American flag and the Christian flag.

The church held a prominent position in my childhood. My

progenitors, who were a founding family of Culpepper, helped build and begin the church. All of my family were married at that altar. We were all baptized and raised in the deep southern beliefs of the church. It had been years, but it still seemed the same. I have always felt at peace when I entered the structure. I still believed. The church was still home.

As I walked into the cemetery behind the church, there were a few other individuals visiting their family members' graves. I walked over to the area enclosed with a white marble wall that protected a larger marker engraved with "Kensington." The marker towered over my ancestors.

While I was a junior at Ole Miss, my eldest brother was diagnosed with testicular cancer. Preston W. Kensington IV was in his late twenties, and we all thought that he had the courage and strength to fight his illness. However, the cancer mocked us all. After several weeks of aggressive therapy, Will lost most of his body weight. But, there seemed to be a glisten of hope in his eyes. He would laugh about our childhood memories and remind me of the joys of our innocence.

After a few months, the hope faded and Will entered into a vegetative state. My mother was always there holding his hand while reading to him. She would take his frail arm and weep and pray to a God in whom she so trusted. I was always amazed at her strength and faith. She would pray unlike any other person I knew. There seemed to be such peace in her voice and actions. She was a beautiful woman, but seeing her hold Will's hand made her angelic.

She never left his side. The nurses brought a portable bed into the room, which my mother used for six weeks. During the first week of January, the physician came into the room and asked the family of our intentions. Will could not breathe on his own. He was not disposing of his bodily waste. His body had essentially stopped functioning. Mother made the decision to remove her son from life-support; it was the toughest decision of her life.

Later on that cold day, the doctor and the respiratory therapist came into the hospital room. His immediate family gathered around the bed. I placed my hand on his leg. Tears began to flow and then it became uncontrollable. Mother held his hand as his soul ascended into Heaven. The Baptist minister was there holding my mother by the shoulders praying within himself. In our own way, we prayed too as we watched the therapist remove the tubes from Will's limp swollen body. The heart monitor stopped. His body shook as his lungs grasped for breath. We too, grasped for breath. Within a few moments, his Heavenly life had begun.

I remember his funeral vividly. The pastor spoke of God's eternal home and the peace of believing in a resurrection. At the end of the sermon, I stood and walked to the grand piano in the front of the church that rested adjacent to the altar. I sat. My hands began to shake. When I started pressing the keys to play *Amazing Grace,* the tears began to fall. I was playing for my brother. There were moments when my eyes were too full of tears to see the keys or the hymnal; I played from memory. I was releasing all the childhood memories that we shared. With each press of the keys, I was releasing Will into eternity.

Will's death caused me to question the true nature of God. I didn't understand how my father was able to live when my brother had to die. I didn't understand why He would allow someone as innocent as Will to die such a horrible death. Why did my mother, the most devout person I knew, have to suffer so much? As I stood there looking at Will's grave, I still questioned. Why did he have to die so early? I needed him. He was my best friend. My mother would say that God needed Will to be an angel to help someone else. I needed my brother.

After visiting my grandparents' and mother's graves, I left First Baptist. I walked the two blocks to Magnolia. When I reached the brick street, I turned left and walked south toward Bronwyn's home. The magnolia trees stood stoically. Many of these trees were over a hundred years old. The people and the events that each could reveal to us amazed me. Before I realized it, I was standing in front of my family home. I hesitantly decided to walk over to the structure. I walked onto the front porch and turned slightly right to walk around the right side of the house to the back porch.

The backyard was a place of solace and peace for me as a child. It was a place to run freely and enjoy childhood. The old Magnolia tree was still standing majestically in the back of the lawn. It was the tree that I fell from and broke my leg. The huge white blossoms reminded me of my lost innocence.

The lawn had just been cut. I stood smelling the grass and reminiscing my childhood. On many hot summer days, I would lie in the grass until the bees and insects chased me away. On one particular morning, I laid in the grass surrounded by the humidity of the hot southern climate. I could hear Shakey singing. He was happy. I jumped up and ran to him as he was walking into the garden. He was smiling from ear to ear.

I loved Shakey. He was an older man whom my parents hired to tend to the lawn and outside maintenance. We called him Shakey because he would just shake for no reason at all. It all began with just a few jitters sporadically. I remember seeing his little finger begin the dance while we were planting flowers in the backyard, right after he was hired. From that moment on, he became Shakey to the Kensington children. We loved him. When the tremors became worse and more prolonged, we realized the cause and how immature and uncaring we were.

On that particular day, Shakey was informed that he was going to be a grandfather. I still remember the joy that radiated from him. I missed the man who taught me compassion and understanding of the less fortunate.

As I stood on the porch, I noticed the same iron swing from my childhood. Every acceptable southern family has an iron swing in the backyard. It is the place where memories were made, where teenage couples kiss. It is the place where grandparents sat while watching children play.

I walked over to the swing. It has remained in the same spot for decades. I sat down. The creaking of the swing rustled the memories in my mind. This swing was an important part of my adolescence. It was the first place I went when I ran away at age 13 because I refused to obey my parents. It was the place where I entered my manhood.

I sat and cried in this exact swing when my dog, Skipper, was hit by a car. He was buried in the corner of the lawn under the Magnolia tree. The methodical groans of the chains grew a little harsher as the years have passed. I sat there for quite some time lost in the retrospection of the cost of being a Kensington.

Being a Kensington required a level of loyalty that could destroy a young child as he grew into adolescence and truly understood how much loyalty was required. We were expected to make our parents proud and to continue the Kensington legacy. I was expected to go to law school at Ole Miss; Blake was expected to be drafted; Sarah Beth was expected to attend college and procreate. In many ways, the loyalty removed our autonomy. It stripped us of our dignity.

As I sat in the old iron swing, I began to sweat from the Mississippi summer heat. It moistened my skin. After living in Virginia for so long, my body was no longer accustomed to the brutal life in Mississippi. The sweat rolled across my forehead, down my nose, and dripped vicariously onto my khaki shorts. It was hot, but I stayed there staring across the lawn at her home. She has lived in the cottage behind our house for all of the years that I have known her. I admired her strength and her grace. I longed to be able to hold her and tell her how sorry I was. I was so sorry for what he did to both of us. I needed her forgiveness.

Ms. Sally

AS I WALKED AROUND THE CORNER, I SAW JACKSON sitting in the swing going back and forth like he was a kid.

"Jackson, what are you doing here? You're supposed to be down the street?"

"Ms. Sally, come give me a hug. I have missed you. How are you?"

"I am good as long as your checks don't bounce."

"Sit with me. Let's catch up."

I sat beside him and we talked for an hour. He's such a good man. I told him all the neighborhood gossip. I told him about all the old women giving their bodies to Corbin, and no one knew about the others. I told him about Mr. Boyce being sick and about to die. He learned about Eric and Emily's business dealings and how she found another man on the side and he doesn't care. I told him about the gold digging woman who just moved into the district two doors down from Mr. Bronwyn's house.

We talked, and I told him everything about our neighbors. We laughed like we did when he was a child. But, he seemed different. Something happened to Jacky when he was in high school. He was always affectionate, but in high school he acted like he had to make me feel better. He was always carrying on like he was taking care of me, instead of me taking care of him. He rarely came home from college. Then, one day he came home, and he told me everything. I could tell the damage was already done. He moved to Virginia, and I rarely saw him again.

After we talked about nearly everyone in Culpepper, he stood and hugged me. We walked to the back porch. Like always, he walked around the house instead of walking through one door and out the other.

Jackson

AFTER LEARNING THE NEIGHBORHOOD GOSSIP, I RE-turned to Bronwyn's home. There was a police officer standing on the front porch talking to my neighbor. I walked up. The woman remained silent while she pointed at me. I paused with a confused expression on my face.

As I walked toward the officer and my accuser, the officer walked toward me, and he asked if I was standing on the porch this morning. I answered appropriately. He continued his inquisition. I answered each of his questions and produced a key to the house. He asked for identification, which I produced. When he noticed my last name, his behavior immediately corrected. He apologized repeatedly as he walked toward his patrol car. The neighbor stood embarrassed. She rejected my invitation for coffee or tea as she slowly retreated into her house.

I walked upstairs to unpack a few more boxes. As I walked down the immense hallway, I noticed the locked door from my childhood. I always wondered what was in that room. One day, Uncle Bronwyn caught me trying to pick the lock with a paper clip. I had no idea what I was doing, but I was determined to enter that room. He yelled at me and sent me home immediately.

It was the moment that I had dreamed of as a child. I ran downstairs and opened the lap drawer from Bronwyn's desk in the library. I clutched the ring of keys and ran upstairs. When I arrived at the door, I inserted the key that was labeled for this use. The door opened easily.

I entered Uncle Bronwyn's attic slowly, and the wind from the door spawned the flight of dust droplets into the sunlight that permeated through the windows. To my surprise, the room was incredibly organized. There were floor to ceiling metal shelving that contained labeled boxes. I walked carefully along the left wall reading the labels. Each label was precise in describing its contents. There were boxes labeled with years and an alphabet. There was a box with an "M" inscribed on a label. There were numerous boxes with names of people whom I did not recognize and their addresses. All of the boxes were covered in dust. When I reached the end of the wall, there were several boxes that were only labeled Big Daddy. There were no other descriptors.

I reached up hesitantly and clutched the top box. Although the boxes were taped shut, time had debilitated the strength of the tape. I tore it open easily. I looked through the box of items from Big Daddy's life. I located a folded piece of paper that contained the order of service for Big Momma's funeral. As I read the words printed, the memories immediately flooded my mind. It had been several years since her passing, and the paper returned me to that day.

The viewing of my grandmother was about to end. Visitation seemed to last a lifetime. I stood and smiled as people entered the room. I recognized most of the people without introducing myself; however, some of the visitors were people from many years ago, people whom I did not know. Big Daddy walked to the catafalque. I decided to join him. We stood there for what seemed like hours. Tears began to fill his eyes, which caused my own eyes to swell. He stood over her and wept. He leaned into the casket and kissed her goodbye.

He squeezed my hand, and with the other hand he lowered the casket shut. He released my hand, turned, and walked away.

On that day, the pastor of First Baptist spoke in solemn tones and declared what a wonderful life Victoria Ann Kensington had lived. The church was packed to capacity. The women from the Magnolia Garden Club were there, as well as the Women's Missionary Union. Tears flowed down everyone's face; especially Big Daddy whom I believed could not cry.

The pastor's words were followed with a burial service in the cemetery behind the church for the family. As we all stood around the hole that never seemed to end, the pastor spoke of an assurance of seeing her again. The casket was lowered slowly into the cold ground. The first shovel of dirt was placed on the casket. We all walked away with tears flowing down our faces. The sadness darkening our worlds. Our matriarch has passed.

Big Daddy met Big Momma after the Second World War. Big Daddy had graduated from Ole Miss and was drafted into the army to serve his country. Big Momma had graduated from Agnes Scott with a literature degree, which was only meant to be used until she was married. She had relatives in Culpepper, and decided to take a teaching job in the town. They met at First Baptist and immediately fell in love.

I am amazed at how long Big Daddy lived. I always thought he would be the first to exit into eternity. He was a man that was known for his bourbon and his tobacco pipe. He was by no means an alcoholic, but he did enjoy a drink before he went to bed every evening while he smoked his pipe. I can still smell the smoke from the many times that I sat on his lap while he read to me. The pipe rested peacefully beside the crystal glass filled with bourbon that sat on the side table in the library. He would always tell us that it helped release him from the day.

I could not imagine burying your soul mate. Yet, he was a strong man. His stories of the war, and how it changed his life forever still resonate in my mind. He would jokingly tell me that he had borrowed a few women while he was in the war. It only cost him a little penicillin.

As I slowly examined the contents of the box, I noticed a shoebox that was wrapped in thick black tape to ensure the protection of the contents. I attempted to open it in the same manner as I had opened the larger container, but I failed. I searched the attic for a tool to help my conquest of the shoebox. I remembered seeing a pair of scissors in a drawer in the parlor. I immediately retrieved the utensils. The amount of tape used slowed the cutting process, but the container finally opened.

Trepidation consumed my mind. Cautiously, I opened the lid. The shoebox was filled with old black and white pictures. Suddenly, I felt sickened. My heart raced. My head swam. My knees buckled.

Sarah Beth

GROWING UP IN CULPEPPER PROVED TO BE A CHAL-
lenging experience. I was different than my siblings. Will was
the mature one. Jackson was the intellectual. Blake was the athlete. I was the shy kid who was always on the outside.

After Gavin and I married, we purchased a home on First
Avenue, not on Magnolia Avenue. Houses a block away were
wonderful dwellings without the enormous prices. Gavin and
I live in a modest five bedroom home with our three children:
Julia, Joseph, and Joshua. Julia was sixteen; Joseph was fourteen,
and Joshua was twelve; though he would physically age, his
mind remained at five years of age.

Jackson has returned to town. He and I talked briefly this
morning, and he invited me over to visit with him and Faulkner.
As I walked onto the front porch, I noticed the precise place-
ments of all of the furniture, even after all of these years. As
I glanced around the porch, I noticed there were small pencil
markings on the porch that indicated where the furniture should
be placed. It was the first time I had noticed the markings. They
reminded me of Uncle Bronwyn's attention to details. I reached

for the doorbell. After a few minutes, I re-sounded the bell. Jackson's Jeep was in the driveway. I opened the door. I called his name as I walked into the foyer, but there was no response.

I repeated my call for my brother. Still no response. I became frantic. I searched the parlor. Nothing. I walked into the kitchen, the den, and the remaining first floor.

I returned to the front of the house. The large staircase was still as beautiful as it was when I was a child. It was on the left wall as one walks through the door in the foyer, opposite the parlor. The hand carved spindles were the focal point of its beauty. The dark wood flooring was mostly covered with a European runner that Bronwyn commissioned. The stairs were five feet wide and reached the fifteen feet distance that connected the first and second floors.

I walked up the stairs. With each step, I called my brother's name. I walked down the hallway on the right. At the end of the hallway, there was an open door, the protected door from our childhood. I ran toward the door and found another set of stairs. Guardedly, I walked up the steps. When I reached the top, I saw Jackson lying on the floor. He was awake but abstracted.

Jackson

WHEN I REVIVED, SARAH BETH WAS STANDING OVER me. Her inquisitive screeching voice engendered a desire to re-enter an unconscious state.

Sarah Beth Kensington was a tall beautiful blonde who attended Agnes Scott like her grandmother had done several decades prior. While there, she majored in English, and once gave thought to becoming a teacher. She was bright and beautiful. However, Sarah Beth refused to live a life controlled by people and ideas with which she did not agree. How she survived to adulthood in the Kensington family should be one of the world's greatest marvels.

Sarah Beth was my oldest sibling. She met Gavin, her husband, in Africa, while in the Peace Corps. She was helping teachers in the school, and Gavin was helping the men with farming in the small village.

When Sarah Beth was courting Gavin, mother was angry. She was angry because Sarah Beth had chosen a Yankee from Boston who attended public school. She often questioned Sarah Beth about finding a nice southern gentleman who was not so abrasive and condescending, perhaps Forrest Wellington, whose family was equal to our own. Sarah Beth knew that Forrest enjoyed the company of other southern gentlemen, so she agreed to date Forrest for a succinct period prior to her engagement to Gavin. Gavin, of course, knew this was happening. It was the first time he realized the type of family into which he was marrying.

Sarah Beth and Gavin loved each other, even though they were very different. Gavin loved red meat, and Sarah Beth was a vegetarian. Sarah Beth loved the opera, and Gavin took great joy in heavy metal music and hard rock and roll. Perhaps, Sarah Beth was taken by Gavin's incredibly handsome nature. He was a tall Italian Catholic who loved to work with his hands. He was not afraid of hard work or manual labor, which was the reason he entered the Peace Corps. His deep brown eyes were the focal point of his face, and those eyes drew Sarah Beth into them each time they stared at each other.

Sarah Beth inquired into my current predicament. I lied to her by telling her that I fainted because of my blood sugar level, though I am not diabetic. She appeared to accept my lie. I asked her to help me up, which she did. I quickly guided her out of the attic. I could not allow her to view the photographs.

In the kitchen, she explained recent events in her life. She was so excited that I was in Culpepper for a year. She always hoped that I would return. We continued to discuss the neighborhood for nearly an hour. She invited me to attend a neighborhood dinner with her on Sunday, which I accepted. She left, and I changed into my running shorts.

Boyce

I KNOW I AM DYING. IT MAY NOT BE TODAY OR NEXT week, but I know. I have had a great life. I'm 84 years old, and I have lived in this house for the past forty years. My Friday five o'clock happy hours with my friends were impeccable. I am not a great cook, but I can make an exquisite martini. I am lonely because no one visits anymore. I gave my life to this town and this neighborhood, and no one stops by to inquire if I am alive or dead. These good Christian people do not give a shit about me. I rely on Meals on Wheels because I can't cook and few of my neighbors share their evening meals.

I say few, but there are two people who do care for me, Auden and Victoria. I am not sure how I would have survived without them. They love me. They genuinely love me. I have been a bastard to Victoria, but she has taken care of me for a few years. She never walks away. She shares her dinner with me. She takes me to medical appointments. And, I have been horribly ugly to her at times. I hope she understands that I really love her too.

I sit on this porch for hours. I use my walker to come out here just to sit and watch the neighbors walk by without saying a word to me. Vivian is the worst of them all. She is on several boards in town, and she pretends to be extremely busy, but I know the truth. She wants everyone to believe that she really cares about the poor. She is an over the top hypocritical liberal. She has been to my house so many times, and I have never been invited to her house. Her husband is somewhat nice, but he never speaks to me when others are around. The Hathaways do speak and have sat with me several times, but most of the others have forgotten me.

I grew up in this neighborhood. Three generations of my family lived in this house and the house next door. My family owned Culpepper Mills, which was one of the largest cotton and wool mills in the state. The mill was operational until the late 70s, and in early 2001, we decided to transform the space into luxury condos. The venture was very profitable, so the old mill name became a real estate investment firm. My nephews and their sons manage the business now, and I rarely see them. I guess I am too old for them too.

Who is that young man running down the street?

"Good afternoon, young man." He stopped.

"Good afternoon to you."

"I have never seen you before in this neighborhood. Who are you?"

"I am sorry?"

"Young man, what do people call you?"

"Most people call me Dr. Kensington."

I was aghast at his wit and his ability to match my own pretentious nature. I was intrigued.

"Come here, young man. Sit with me for a moment. So, who are your people?"

Dr. Kensington spoke briefly of his childhood on Magnolia, and I realized who he was. He continued discussing his current reasons for returning to Culpepper. I knew his parents. His grandparents were legendary in this town, possibly the state. I knew his uncle Bronwyn. I knew more about this young man than he knew that I knew. We talked for a few minutes, and he agreed that we would spend more time together later in the week.

Jackson's mother and I were close friends, though I was not a fan of his father. His father was an asshole to anyone who could not advance his career. But, we did humor each other for Elizabeth's sake. She was such a stunning woman; she was incredibly well bred. My father and her father were business associates. I was still amazed that Elizabeth would marry him.

Jackson left as abruptly as he arrived. I decided to exit the humid Mississippi heat. I grasped my walker and raised my body. Slowly, I shuffled to the doorway. I raised my right foot and placed it on the threshold. My left foot raised and landed next to my right. I was tired. I continued into the house and used my left hand to reach behind me to close the front door.

With each push of the walker, my feet slowly followed. It was time to take my medicine that was on my bedside table. I made it into my bedroom, sat on the bed, and pushed the walker away from me. I swallowed my medicine and realized the walker was untouchable. I reached for it, but it was too far. I raised my body from the bed. I stepped toward the walker. My knees gave way, and I slid down the side of my bed. My ass hit the floor. I sat trapped in my own abandoned existence. I reached for the walker, but it was too far. I tried a second time, again, too far.

The anger began to rise within me. God why don't you

just bring me home. Why did you take him from this world so quickly? Why God? Why am I sitting on this damn floor trapped? That damn walker, this damn old body that doesn't work anymore. Damn it. Just damn it all. Why God? Why am I suffering so much?

The tears began to roll down my cheeks. I cried. I missed my youth. I missed my friends. I reached again, hoping my arms could do it. I imagined my fingers were longer. My arms too thin and frail to stretch the distance. I imagined in some miraculous way that God would bring it to me. I hoped He would. But, there were no angels or help from him. I gave up. I sat on the floor hopeless as my body released more fluid from itself.

Jackson

I RUN DAILY. IT CLEARS MY MIND AND HELPS ME FO-cus. Running is my day time bourbon. Today was perfect for running. I needed to dispel the photographs that I viewed in the attic, but I couldn't. Those images were now engrained in my soul.

Big Daddy was wearing a Grand Wizard gown. He was kicking and beating a black man while holding a torch, waiting for the moment to place the flames on the young man's skin. Big Daddy and the mob of white robed men had pulled the young Freedom Riders off a bus during a bus ride through the segregated south. There were other pictures of him leading a mob of Klan members in marches through Birmingham. There was an article from the *Birmingham News* that discussed a church bombing that killed four children. I was afraid that he was connected to their deaths. There was a picture of Big Daddy tying a young black man to the bumper of a car. My soul ached.

There were so many pictures of the most influential man in my life filled with hatred. As I ran, I started to tear up. The man who taught me how to fish and to hunt was a racist. Big Daddy held me when I hated my parents. We sat in the swing eating to-mato sandwiches laughing at the silliness of the dog. He spoiled me. He held me when I needed the strength of his huge hands around me. Everyone knew that I was his favorite. I questioned how such a dichotomy could exist in a single soul.

My mind raced. The thoughts seemed uncontrollable. I ran. I ran faster. My mind ran along side of me. I tried to run faster, but it kept pace. I came to Culpepper to write, not to be con-sumed by the dark family secrets. Secrets destroy relationships; they destroyed my family. I thought it would be easier to face my past, but the realities of my past and the reasons I left Culpepper were surfacing. I was not sure about this decision anymore. Per-haps I should have stayed in Virginia, or gone to another place that was not filled with the memories that engendered so much hatred in my life.

This morning, my grandfather's sins slapped me across the face. I loved him. He was my rock. Now, I know. We can never truly know anyone. There will always be a part of someone into which we will never be able to glimpse. I thought he was an honorable and loving man. Instead, he was a horrible racist who took pleasure in hurting people who were not like him. I wonder what he would have done to my little brother. Would he have thrown him to the ground and beat him with a bat because he was something that my grandfather abhorred, something that the Klan rejected? I ran lost in my own anger and hatred. The same anger that I had for my father was projecting to my grand-father. I was ashamed to be a Kensington. I was ashamed to be from Culpepper. Together, we ran side by side, unable to escape the other.

I was lost in my own anger when an older man sitting on

his porch hindered my run by beckoning me to join him on his porch. His hair was gray; his arms and legs frail and weak. His long fingers seemed to only be bone covered in a thin layer of white skin. A gray metal walker rested near him, with yellow tennis balls covering the two back feet. He invited me to sit with him for a few moments. I sat with him long enough to cure his curiosity of me. He knew my family and apparently my uncle quite well. When speaking of Bronwyn, the old man seemed melancholy, which engendered my own inquisitive impulses.

After our visit, I returned to the hard red bricks of Magnolia Avenue. I ran south for three blocks then turned left and headed toward First Avenue. The houses on First were substantially smaller, but they remained appropriate for the Culpepper Historic District. The original baked red clay was covered with asphalt years ago. I ran by Sarah Beth's home. She was sitting in the front lawn while Joshua swung in the tire swing. She waved, and I returned the gesture as I continued north on First Avenue.

I was always amazed at Sarah Beth being able to raise a child with special needs. Joshua would remain locked in the mind of prepubescent child, though his body would age, his mind would remain at the same innocent age. He would always enjoy flying in the tire swing or pretending to be Superman. The innocence of childhood could not be ripped from his soul. Sometimes, I longed for the same peace in my life. Sarah Beth also showed me that I would not be a good father. She and Gavin are raising three wonderful kids. I have seen her interactions with each of her children, and it has revealed my own selfishness. I am far too egocentric to be a father. In all honesty, I am surprised that Faulkner is still alive.

After a few blocks, I saw the same young man who spoke

to me the this morning. He was exiting a house on the right. When I reached the driveway of the home, a stunningly beautiful woman in her fifties stepped outside of the door with a covered dish and began walking to the black Audi parked in the driveway. She was tall and slender, and her black hair flowing in the slight breeze was held back with a pair of Chanel sunglasses. Her chiseled calf muscles showed radiantly below the hem of her Lilly Pulitzer dress. The white dress, which fit her well, was covered in large ornate flowers and was accented by a pair of Manolos. She carried herself with poise and confidence.

My curiosity rose when I saw her. She was a beautiful woman, and I assume the young man was her son. We made eye contact. I waved and smiled.

The Mississippi sun was hot. I continued running to erase the images of Big Daddy from my mind, knowing that it was impossible. The sun was burning my chest. Suddenly, I heard a boisterous sound of thunder rage through the blue sky. The water fell like ammunition, hard bullets of water leaving indentations in the dry soil. The droplets striking my red skin causing it to burn more intensely. I ran slower, allowing the wetness to cover me, to cool me. After a few minutes, the storm passed, a rainbow appeared, and the smell of the rain intoxicated me. It reminded me of my childhood and the joy of running in the backyard as it rained. The droplets rolling down our half naked bodies. We ran, laughed, being chased by the innocence of our youth. The dirt smell filling our souls.

Joshua

ZOOM. ZOOM. ZOOM. FLYING HIGHER AND HIGHER. Look at that little ant walking through the grass. What a beautiful little ant. I think he is lost. Zoom. Zoom. Zoom. I am going to fly down and save that ant. He needs me. He is lost. The ant is lost. Zoom. He is going to die. The old man who sits on his porch and yells at me sometimes. He is not being mean. Mommy says he is lonely. He yells at me because he wants me to talk to him. Mommy talks to him. He tells me not to run on his porch. He doesn't want me to fall and get hurt. He is going to die because he is sick. Sometimes sick people die. My dog was sick and he died. Sometimes sick people die. The old man on the porch is going to die because he is sick. I don't see the ant. He made it home to his friends and his mommy and daddy and Big Daddy and Big Momma. Zoom. Zoom. Zoom.

Aubrey

CORBIN STOPPED BY THIS AFTERNOON FOR A QUICK visit. I could never date such a young man. I am double his age, but we both understand the parameters and the purposes for our meetings.

As I left, I noticed a man running up First Avenue. He waved, and I responded appropriately. I have never seen him in the neighborhood before, but because the Army post is so close, he is probably a new soldier.

I have been married three times. Honestly, I am afraid to be alone. I am afraid to die alone in that house. I could lie in that house for a few days before anyone realized that I was dead. I know Corbin and I will never marry, but his presence gives the peace that as long as he is around that I am not completely alone. As a little girl, my mother always told me that the right handsome man would come along and marry me. But, I had to be a good wife and take care of him. It was up to me to take care of the house and to make him happy or he would find someone else who did a better job. She always told me to make sure that I was doing my very best so no one could ever replace me.

As I pulled up into his driveway, Boyce was absent from his normal chair on the porch. I walked up the steps to his front porch. I rang the bell while holding the dish in my right hand. He did not respond. I reached up to a designated spot above the door frame, where Boyce always placed a key, especially after the last fall that caused him to be hospitalized. He had fallen and laid in the floor for two days because Auden and Victoria were out of town. It was obvious that Boyce was not recovering from his recent illness. He was simply progressing through the aging process.

The key was not needed. I opened the door and called his name. Silence returned through the stale cold air. Boyce's home was always perfect. Ms. Sally was taking wonderful care of him. I walked into the kitchen and placed the casserole in his icebox. I returned to the front of the home, and cautiously walked toward Boyce's bed chambers.

"Boyce are you decent honey? I am coming in," I called out.

"Go away. I am not accepting any callers this afternoon," he responded.

"Boyce, I am coming in to check on you." I walked into his room. He was sitting on the floor. He had attempted to stand up without his walker, which caused him to slide down the side of his bed. "Boyce, my goodness, honey."

I bent over to lift him up. His boney hand made a sudden and deep impact with my face, while he screamed, "I told you not to come in here. Why are you even in my house? Did you bring me some of your shitty food again? Aubrey, I don't want your horrible food anymore. And, I don't need your help. Get out!"

I stood, turned, and walked away. I left Boyce on the floor

trapped by his own pride. The tears began to roll down my face. I ran out of the house, leaving the front door ajar. Ms. Sally was walking up the steps.

"Ms. Aubrey, you alright?"

I did not wish to respond. I simply wanted to be away from the experience. I sat in my car with the tears still present. The pain of his hand was beginning to surface on my face in a swollen and bruised manner.

I am not sure why I was so surprised. Boyce has made me cry numerous times, but then he would send flowers apologizing for his barbaric behavior. Boyce was a prideful man, and any help from anyone whom he perceived as an equal was not tolerated.

When he was younger, he was stunningly handsome, and the young army men thought so as well. Boyce loved the company of younger military men, but he loved appropriate appearances even more. He did not want his neighbors to know of his actions, especially his Magnolia Avenue neighbors. His home rested on a double lot, thus, one could walk directly out of his backdoor and continue walking several yards to First Avenue. Years ago, Boyce had the entire back lawn enclosed in 12 feet wooden fencing, which increased the privacy of his encounters. Army soldiers would park on First Avenue, walk through a 12-foot wooden gate and continue across his back lawn and enter through his backdoor.

To this day, he believed that most people in the district were not aware of his sexual happenings, but we all knew. In those days, sex between men was taboo in the south, especially in Mississippi and among the elitist citizens of the district. Boyce's family was one of the wealthiest families in Mississippi. For generations, they owned one of the largest cotton mills in the state. His family would have excommunicated him if they found out about him. Soldiers could be discharged for engaging in such risqué behaviors, but Boyce had hundreds of visitors over the years. It was his secret, shielded by the cloak of southern arrogance.

Jackson

THE MASSIVE PIPE ORGAN REVERBERATED THROUGH the space, welcoming our minds and our souls into worship. The sanctuary was a beautiful place. There were two columns on each side of the choir loft that connected the floor to the ceiling. The golden pipes for the organ were behind the choir loft, and they seemed to reach into the heavens. There were nine chandeliers that hung twenty feet from a trey ceiling. The sanctuary floor was divided into three sections of pews, with twenty-five pews in each section.

My eyes began to trace the depictions of the gospels on the stained glass windows that guarded the sanctuary. The deep dark colors revealed the beauty of Christ's life. The church was a beautiful monstrosity. I sat in the balcony above the congregation.

The sanctuary was always a place of peace for me. As a child, I sat in the pew next to my mother and father every Sunday and every Wednesday. Church was a place where I truly learned the power of love and what it meant to unconditionally love someone. I was a devout believer. Then, I discovered the true ugliness of my father, a man who said he loved God too. He had given so much money to this congregation over the years. What if they knew? It crushed me. The truth of the egotism of humanity crushed my soul. I attempted to create my own reasons why God would allow such things to happen. I questioned why I had to be the one to uncover the truth and why that truth needed to be buried within my spirit. Why had He chosen me to shield the truth? A few years later, I left for college and started hiding the truth. I thought Maggie was the person who could bring true healing to my spirit, but my family hindered it.

I still loved God, but the questions have become more profound within me. I didn't understand His plan for my life. Although I knew it was not possible, I felt disconnected from Him and what He wanted to do in my life. But, even in the disconnection, I continued going to church. I continued attempting to find Him. I wanted Him to tell me why. I needed His voice to calm me.

When I graduated from Ole Miss with an English degree, my father expected me to attend law school. Indeed, he had already made the necessary phone calls for me to be accepted, regardless of my LSAT score. I didn't want to be an attorney. When I told him I was entering Alabama's PhD program in English, he scoffed at my decision. It was the first time in my life that I refused to do what he instructed.

We were in the library when I disclosed my intentions. He immediately reached for his bourbon. His hand began shaking because of his anger. Droplets of the light brown liquid jumped from the glass and splattered on the oak wood flooring below. His voice mocked my intellectualism. As he screamed at me, I politely excused myself. Mother ran into the library to calm him, as she always did. I walked the two blocks to Second Avenue.

When I reached the church, I opened the door. I walked through the vestibule through another set of large mahogany doors, which led into the sanctuary. Quietly, I sat on the last pew. I was scared and angry. I was scared of my father. I was scared of making the wrong decision. I sat searching for peace and certainty, which I found in the calmness of the sanctuary.

The voices in the choir refocused my attention. My viewing repositioned to the individuals seated in the pews below me, between the windows. I saw Auden and Victoria, the couple who cared for Boyce daily. I recognized the woman walking to her black Audi. As my eyes surveyed the gathering of souls, I saw, embedded in the people, other neighbors who had rejected Boyce in his last days. They refused to share their suppers, even when Victoria told the neighbors Boyce needed meals. A simple small serving of a casserole for an old dying man was too much to share for these neighbors. As he sat alone on his porch and stared into the loneliness of the neighborhood, his neighbors did not stop and sit with him. Instead, they ignored the needs of one of their former friends.

Many of these neighbors had engaged with Boyce in his younger days. Some of them visited his famous Friday martini hours. They attended supper club gatherings with him and attended his elaborate Christmas parties. Now, the same neighbors he broke bread with in his youth sat in the church, while he sat alone in the pain of loneliness and rejection.

As the pianist began to play *Blessed Assurance*, a soloist began giving life to the words. As she sang, I remembered my mother. She loved God. Every Sunday, she was seated on the seventh pew on the far right of the church. She was always dressed in church appropriate attire, which every southerner is taught from an early age. She was impeccable in every aspect of her life, especially her faith. She believed more than anyone I knew.

She was a rose growing among so many briars. Her faith was unshakeable. During my brother's illness, her belief in the unseen grew. It was her faith that led her to anonymously donate money to the homeless shelter. She volunteered for numerous organizations because she truly loved the ones others rejected. Her faith was strong. I missed her.

Mother grew up outside of Tupelo, Mississippi. Her father was a banking genius, and her mother earned a nursing degree, which she used only during the war. Elizabeth Bradford was slender and radiant all of her life. Her smile captivated any room she entered. She contained an innate level of grace and poise that could not be learned. For most of her life, her deep brown hair was always shoulder length, maintained with weekly appointments at the hair parlor. When her hair started to gray, she wore it with confidence and pride.

Elizabeth, attended Wesleyan College, the oldest college for women in the country. While there, she majored in Art History, with a particular interest in neoclassical art because of its connections to classical thought. After college, Elizabeth returned home and began working in one her father's bank branches in Jackson, Mississippi. Two years after graduation, she met my father through a social function sponsored by the Junior League, of which she was a member. When they married, she resigned from her employment and began a family and a life with Preston W. Kensington, III.

I was teaching in Virginia when my mother died. It was the darkest day of my life. As a child, I would dream that she died. I would wake in a cold sweat and run across our house on

Magnolia to my parent's bedroom. I would scream, "Mommy, please don't die. Please don't die." She would hold me until I was calm, then she would walk me back to my bedroom, holding me until I fell asleep. I was afraid of a life without her.

I was teaching a class in southern literature when my cell phone rang. It was odd that Sarah Beth called during the day; she knew my class schedule. I excused myself and retreated into the hallway. Sarah Beth gave me the news. Our mother was standing in the kitchen when her heart stopped. She fell face forward onto the marble floor. There was no bruising, so the physician said that it was immediate. She felt no pain. I was numb. I sat in the hallway until one of my students came outside to check on me. I motioned for them to leave the class.

My mother's death was a small reminder of God's grace. My mother died instantly. She never suffered. There were numerous moments when I believed that God was rewarding her for the sins of my father. Those moments gave me hope.

As the hymn ended, the pastor's voice reverberated through the speakers and beckoned for my attention.

Michael

GOOD MORNING. WELCOME TO FIRST BAPTIST. WE ARE so glad you are here this morning. If you are visiting with us, please make yourself at home. We are glad that you are here. If you need anything, please locate an usher. Today's scripture reading is Matthew 22: 34-40. But when the Pharisees had heard that he had put the Sadducees to silence, they were gathered together. Then one of them, which was a lawyer, asked him a question, tempting him, and saying, Master, which is the greatest commandment in the law? Jesus said unto him, Thou shalt love the Lord thy God with all thy heart, and with all thy soul, and with all thy mind. . This is the first and great commandment. And the second is like unto it, Thou shalt love thy neighbor as thyself. On these two commandments hang all the law and the prophets.

I learned something a few years ago from a young lady who attended our church before she and her husband were re-stationed at Fort Henderson. Whenever she walked by another person, she always made a statement complimenting the person and then asked, "How are you today?" And, she would wait for a response. Julie was incredibly interested in engaging with everyone. One day, I asked her why she did that, and she responded, "Because we never know how people really feel on the inside, and how our encouragement may affect them. Christ told us to love our neighbor, and that involves connecting with people. We need to show people that we are interested in their lives, pastor."

Perhaps, Julie was correct, the greatest act of love is simply connecting to people where they are in their lives.

People assume that the charge that Christ gave us in this scripture is simple and easy. Many over the years have stated, "I love you" in a very flippant and nonchalant manner. In many ways, "I love you" has developed into a cliché equal to "goodbye" or "have a nice day." But, the type of love that Christ speaks of in this text grows from a sincere desire to have a personal relationship with God and others. It is a dedicated love. A reverent love. A loyal love.

Notice Christ first says to love "the Lord your God with all of your heart, your soul, and your mind." This is not the flippant "I love you" that many of us say on a daily basis. This is a fervent and holy love that includes all aspect of the human condition. It means loving God with our whole consciousness. It is a love that is engrained in our humanity through a personal relationship with God.

Secondly, the love that Christ speaks of in the first commandant engenders the love of the second commandment. You can't love people the way Christ desires us to love people, if you first don't love God the way that he instructs. The love that is embedded in this scripture is one of purity, of power, of unselfish dedication to a higher purpose. It is a love that requires a personal relationship and the recognition that we need and love God because of who He is, not what He can provide for us. I am going to say that again. We love God because of who He is, not what He can provide for us.

We must understand the idea of a self-love and what that means in our understanding of loving people. Most of us in this sanctuary have loved ourselves over others in our neighborhoods. We have loved our needs over the needs of our neighbors. We have loved our friends' needs over the needs of the stranger. In many cases, we must deny ourselves in order to truly love others the way that God wants us to love people. He has called us to love people.

We live in a tumultuous world. It is a world where we have placed a priority on meeting our own needs over those of the poor, the sick, and the out casted. We live in a world where people are not loved because they are poor, homeless, sick, or because they are simply different. Christ calls us to love everyone; there is no exception. If we are going to love in the manner that Christ wants us to love, there can be no conditions or stipulations to receive our love.

We don't love people because of what they have done to us or to others. We are human, and there are times in our lives when our neighbors hurt us; they reject us, and they do horrible things us. But, the type of love that Christ discusses here is one that requires us to love people where they are. Our neighbors are all in different seasons and spaces in their lives. We must love them where they are.

As we conclude today, the question is raised, "how do you love others?" Is it a love that is conditioned upon a race, a class, a social status? Is it a love that is conditioned on a behavior? Perhaps, we all need to reflect on how we love everyone.

Please stand if you are able. The doors of the church are open if you feel God is leading you to become part of this church family.

Sarah Beth

I WALKED OVER TO UNCLE BRONWYN'S HOUSE TO WALK
with Jackson to the Sunday Supper Club, which is a huge deal
in the district. Each family in the club is responsible for hosting
dinner on a Sunday once a month. The calendar is developed
yearly. This Sunday it was held at Auden and Victoria's home,
which was on the north side of Magnolia. Their home was one of
the larger homes in the district. It was designed by Levi Weeks.
The structure was a two story red brick home. There were two
rows of eight floor-to-ceiling windows across the front of the
home. Four large white columns were centered in the front of
the home, protecting the massive entryway, leaving three windows on each side of the home open for splendid views of Magnolia. The four columns also supported a second floor balcony.

We walked up to the entrance, rang the bell, and waited for
our hosts. Auden opened the door and introduced himself to
Jackson. He hugged and kissed my cheek. We walked through
the home and noticed the exquisite paintings of their progenitors.
The large oak staircase was in the center of the foyer and opened
like a huge fan as it reached from the first floor to the second.

Victoria hired Ms. Sally and Mr. Jim to help with the event. Ms. Sally was my second mother. They were wonderful people. I loved them dearly. They had worked for most of the families in the district.

We walked through the foyer into the back of the house. The gathering was on the back lawn. As we walked outside, the beauty of their garden was breath taking. Victoria had truly created a spectacular event, as she was known for doing.

Jackson and I walked around the lawn, and I introduced him to the neighbors. He met Eric and Emily, a middle age couple who earned their wealth from buying gas stations around the state. They were both shorter individuals, with brown eyes and brown hair. Neither were from old Culpepper families, which meant nothing to me but was everything to so many of the district citizens.

Jackson met Elizabeth and Patrick, who are my favorite people in the district. Elizabeth is old money and to the manor born. She attended Ole Miss and majored in Philosophy because she found it interesting. Because of her social status, a degree was never meant to be used; it was only needed to continue to legitimize her acceptance in the southern aristocracy. Patrick was also to the manor born, only from Jackson, Mississippi, which was 45 minutes east of Culpepper. They met while at Ole Miss. They married when they graduated then Patrick attended medical school.

Jackson and I continued to maneuver through the gathering. He met Cara and Aubrey, all of which were enamored by his classic looks and intelligence. Aubrey mentioned noticing Jackson running on First Avenue the other day. Phoebe invited him to coffee one day this week.

Dinner was phenomenal. Victoria was by far the best chef in all of Culpepper. We began dinner with a classic Soupe à l'oignon or if one chose, Roquefort cheese with numerous crackers and breads. The main course was a Bouillabaisse of fresh fish, or if one preferred, she had also prepared a Coq au vin and a duck confit, all of which smelled amazing. For dessert, I chose the Crème brûlée, but she had also prepared a Tarte Tatin, which is basically caramelized fruits in lots of sugar and butter.

I think some of the neighbors are jealous of Victoria. It is obvious that Emily wants to be just like Victoria. If you watch closely, you can see how Emily has started to adopt some of her mannerisms. I have been involved in several community meetings outside of the district where Emily would mention being friends with Victoria. Also, Vivian is a wonderful cook, but she is not as polished, and she seems to hold the most animosity toward Victoria. Conversely, Elizabeth and Victoria are cut from the same cloth. They have been friends for years. They are on the same charity boards and the same book clubs. I love them both, and if I were concerned with social status in Culpepper, I would emulate both of them.

The meal reminded Jackson and me of our childhood trips to France. Those were some of the greatest moments of my childhood. It was one of our mother's favorite countries. She enjoyed staying in small French towns outside of Paris. She refused to stay in a hotel in Paris as my father wanted, rather she chose to rent a small house in a small town for three to four weeks. I am still shocked that my father would leave his practice for so long, but he did. He did a lot for her. We were immersed in the normal French culture, not the Paris upper class culture connected to tourism.

After dinner, Jackson walked me home. We sat in the front yard. The lawn glowed with the radiance of a mass of lightning bugs nearby. We both laughed out loud because it had been years since we caught the magical creatures and placed the bugs into mason jars with holes in the lid. We would lock the bugs in the jar and stare at them for hours. As we sat there, Joshua jumped up from the ground and walked a few feet away; he unzipped his pants and relieved himself in the front lawn. When he was done, he ran to the tire swing and began to pretend he was superman.

Although I am older, I admired Jackson. I was proud that he was able to leave Culpepper. He was able to leave the family business and create a separate existence for himself. I was proud of him when he refused to go to law school. Our father was never the same after that moment. It was intense the first few years when Jackson would come home from Alabama, where he was completing his PhD. It was so intense that his visits decreased over his time there. When he graduated, he moved to Virginia and only came home a few times a year. After mother died, he rarely came home. It has been years since he has been here.

As we stared into the darkness, the flickering of the bugs lessened. Joshua was asleep in the grass. He loved the grass. He loved to roll in the grass creating green stains in all of his clothes. His favorite thing was sleeping with Brick in the middle of the day while the hot sun fell on them. He found comfort there.

The dew was falling. We sat quietly listening to each other in the stillness. We laughed about the silliness of our childhood. Jackson knew he was the favorite child growing up. We all knew it too. He used it to his advantage whenever he could. I, on the other hand, was the outcast of the clan. I was the oldest so I am sure it was because of the first child syndrome. Also, being the only girl in the midst of three brothers also caused problems. Our parents told me, "They are boys. It's the way they were created. You're a girl. You're different."

As we sat there laughing at our memories, an owl called into the darkness. The air became more tolerable. The wetness of the night surrounded us.

It was good for me to see him. We sat in the darkness enjoying the quietness of it all. I missed my family. I missed having a sibling who understood me. I missed the sibling connection. Honestly, I was not sure why I stayed here so long. My parents and grandparents were gone. I was the only Kensington here, but it still felt like home.

Boyce

I'VE BEEN SITTING IN THIS PARLOR ALL DAY. VICTORIA came to visit at noon and left me lunch. Ms. Sally came to give me a bath and said that she would return later to check on me. I just wish it was over. I am not afraid to die. I am afraid to die alone. I do not want Victoria or anyone to walk in here and find me dead in my bed. I need someone to hold my hand as I leave this world. I need that. I pray that every day. Please God, grant me that one desire. He died in his bed with someone beside him. We had a wonderful night playing the piano and drinking martinis. At some point in the night, he died. When I woke up, his cold lifeless hand was wrapped around my hand. He went in peace, and I deserved the same.

"Thank you for bringing me supper, after the way I acted a few days ago. Will you sit with me for a few minutes?"

"Of course, honey. How are you feeling?"

"Honestly, Aubrey, I am tired. I am not getting better."

"You are. You have good days. I have seen you. You're going to be better soon."

"I am not going to get better. And, I need you."

JOSEPH R. JONES

"What do you need, honey?"

"At some point, I am going to want to leave this life. I do not want to suffer. I don't want a prolonged death. I don't want to die alone."

"Boyce, what are you asking me?"

"When I am ready, I want you to help me die with dignity and grace."

"I can't do that, Boyce. I just can't. No, I won't do it."

"Yes, you can. I am trusting you. Please. I need it Aubrey. I can't die alone. Please."

I took her hand into mine. Huge tears began to fall from her eyes. She was a beautiful woman. The Chanel sunglasses were holding her hair perfectly around her face. Her mascara began streaking. She squeezed my hand softly. I loved her belief that tomorrow would be a better day. She really believed that I was going to get better. She knew that she would come over in a few weeks and all would be back to normal. She believed her hope would comfort me and help me stand up from this sofa and walk. I loved that about Aubrey. In the most painful times, she had an incredibly unwavering faith that God would heal and restore.

"You're going to get better."

"No, I won't. I know that. I just know it."

"What do you want me to do?"

"When the time comes, a physician friend has given me a syringe. Release the liquid into my arm. Remove the syringe and hold my hand as I leave. Just please remember to hold my hand."

"Boyce, I can't. I just can't."

She stood and hugged me. I could feel her body shaking.

She kissed my forehead and told me that she loved me. She loved me even after the way I treated her. She still loved me, and I knew that she loved me. She walked to the door, turned, and said goodnight.

Aubrey

I PULLED THE DOOR CLOSED. TEARS STILL IN MY EYES. I couldn't do what he asked me to do. I could never be the reason anyone died. As I pulled the door, Michael opened the black iron wrought gate and walked up the sidewalk toward the steps.

"Hello, Aubrey. How are you?"

"Hey, Pastor. I am good, despite the tears ruining my make-up right now."

"I am sorry. How is he?"

"He's himself. Go in. I am sure he would love to see you."

He reached and hugged me. It comforted me. Michael was the city's pastor. Everyone loved him. He calmed me when I needed it. He heard my fears and helped me see the hand of God in my life when I could not see it on my own. I am glad he was here with Boyce.

When I was in college, I was at a fraternity party. We were all drinking. I was young, but I knew better. One of the college frat boys invited me up to his room. I glanced at my friends who used their eyes and nods to give me permission to go upstairs. He was handsome with brown hair and brown eyes. He started kissing me softly, like any girl would want; but then he became aggressive. I told him no. I told him I needed to go find my friends. I started crying, but my tears did not stop him.

When he was done, he stood, pulled up his pants, and told me that I could clean up in the bathroom. He walked downstairs. I sat in that room and cried. I walked to the bathroom washed him off of me and prepared to walk downstairs. I hid what happened to me that night. No one would ever find out. A few weeks later, I discovered that I was pregnant. I made an appointment in Birmingham. On a Thursday, I drove there because I knew that no one would recognize me. I did not want anyone to ever know of my sin.

When I left the clinic, I drove the entire way to my dorm crying and begging God to forgive what I had done. I cried the entire distance, while promising Him that I would never do it again, no matter what happened in my life.

I just don't think that I can do it for Boyce. I can't take another life. I can't do that to my soul.

The tears were still present as I pulled into my driveway.

Jackson

WHEN I RETURNED TO BRONWYN'S HOUSE, I WALKED into the parlor and toward the bar. It was a beautiful room with solid dark wood panels covering the walls. I reached up and opened the liquor cabinet. I chose the appropriate Waterford glass. I reached for the Woodford Reserve Double Oaked bourbon. Carefully, I poured the honey amber liquid into the class. The smell of tranquility rose into my nostrils.

I don't drink before five in the evening because I want to always be in control of my drinking, which is what a good southern man is taught. I also don't drink to inebriation; I am measured and precise in my drinking. My grandfather taught me that. In high school, he brought me into the library and poured two bourbons, one he pulled to his lips, the other he handed to me. As I shook my head and said, "No thank you," his stern eyes reprimanded my decline. I reached for the glass.

"Jacky, you need to learn now how to control your alcohol. You must control it so it doesn't control you. You are never to drink more than three drinks in public. People will talk Jacky, and their perception is society's reality. But, most important,

Jacky, is that you do not drink to get drunk; instead you drink it to enjoy the process. It takes a very special process to create something such as this. The process always matters. Never waste it on drunkenness. Does that make sense, son?"

I remember nodding my head, but not truly understanding what he meant. I made it through a quarter of the drink before I knew I should stop.

I glanced toward the Steinway that has rested silent in that room for years. Uncle Bronwyn played, but more importantly, the piano was necessary for appearances, which are the cornerstone of southern culture.

The piano was beautiful. I raised the black lid. I sat down and noticed the Baptist Hymnal rested quietly and patiently. I opened to one of my mother's favorite hymn, *There Is a Fountain.* I positioned my hands on the white keys, and began pressing the notes. The hymn came to life. My fingers perfectly caressed the keys in a loving and respectful manner. The music flowed upward to her heavenly ears. In that moment, I knew she was listening. I knew she was there.

As I continued to play, tears began to wash the keys. Those were my tears of remembrance. They were my tears of hatred toward a man who destroyed the life of a woman in a home a few blocks away. A home into which I struggled walking. When I was a child, Ms. Sally was our full time nanny, and she lived in the two bedroom cottage behind the house. Each morning she made sure we were fed and ready for school. She spanked us when we needed it. She held us when we were crying. In many ways, she was our mother. She was the second most influential woman in my life. I loved her.

On a cold winter day when I was in high school, I returned

home from school because I wasn't feeling well. I entered the house, and called for Ms. Sally. I heard no response. I searched throughout the house as quickly as I could, but found nothing. I assumed she was in the cottage. I walked out the backdoor and across the lawn to Ms. Sally's house. When I was about to knock on the door, I heard her crying. I hesitated. I listened. I walked over to a window where the drapes were open. Cautiously, I crouched in the bushes and peered into the window attempting to not be noticed. She was laying on the bed naked, and my father was atop her thrusting violently. There was a look of shear aggression on his face. She cried as quietly as possible. Her tears did not affect him.

I turned and ran away. I ran as fast as possible to Uncle Bronwyn's. I was a slim teenage nerdy boy. I regret leaving. I have held that secret inside of my soul for many years. It haunted my mind. My father raped Ms. Sally. It was not just once; that monster hurt Ms. Sally repetitively over the years. She was scared to tell anyone. He was a very powerful man whose grandfather was once the governor of Mississippi.

Father scared us both. He was a domineering man. There were rumors around the state that he rarely lost a court case in his twenty years of practicing the law. He became one of the youngest state Supreme Court judges because of his political connections and his money. I am convinced that I received a passing grade in a few college courses because the professor discovered who my father was, The Honorable Preston William Kensington, III.

He demanded a level of loyalty from people, especially family. As children, we were taught loyalty is the most important attribute of being a respectable man. I knew that if I spoke of this horror to any human, the wrath of Preston Kensington would fall upon me because I would have broken family loyalty, especially because he never saw Ms. Sally as family. To him, she was a woman my mother hired. Too, I was afraid of losing his pride in me. I was afraid he would stop loving me.

At the time, I believed those things were more important than Ms. Sally, the loving woman who cared for me when I was sick. She cared for me without the judgmental glare of a southern mother. I loved her. I hated looking into her eyes. I knew the pain reverberating in her soul, without her knowing that I knew.

When I was nineteen, I came home from Ole Miss unexpectedly on a Friday afternoon. I walked into the house and Ms. Sally was cleaning the kitchen from preparing lunch. I knew we were alone. Mother was at the Magnolia Club, and Father was in Jackson. After a few minutes, I told her what I witnessed. She began crying. I held her as she once held me, tightly and protective. She wept on my shoulders. Later, she told me of the countless abortions for which he paid. If she refused to handle the situation, we both knew he would solve the problem.

Bourbon helped ease those memories. It dulled the edges of the sword that pierced me each time I saw Ms. Sally or my father. I loved her. I loved her as much as I loved my own mother. In so many ways, I am who I am because of her.

The notes from the hymnal were no longer visible. The tears clouded my sight. My voice followed the keys. *The dying thief rejoiced to see, That fountain in his day; And there may I, though vile as he, wash all my sins away: Wash all my sins away. Wash all my sins away. And there may I, though vile as he, Wash all my sins away.*

Victoria

I ARRIVED AT BOYCE'S EARLY ON MONDAY. I INSERTED my key and opened the door slowly, while calling his name. He did not respond. I walked into his bedroom, where I found Ms. Sally giving him a sponge bath.

"Ok, Mr. Boyce, I got to wash your balls," she told him.

"Go ahead. No one has touched them in years."

I smiled at his humor, even in his despair. I walked through the house to the kitchen. As I walked, I smiled at all of the Broadway Theatre Posters that were displayed throughout his home. *Godspell, Grease, A Cat on a Hot Tin Roof, Fiddler on the Roof*, and so many more. Boyce enjoyed Broadway and New York City.

The white grand piano that he stopped playing years ago sat alone and unwanted. Boyce never explained why he stop playing; he simply never touched the keys again. He refused to sell it because he believed that all acceptable southerners must have a piano in their house, even if the keys and pedals were never pressed. Southern rules were important to Boyce.

I walked through his library. The room was magnificent. He

had read every book in this hallowed room. Before he became ill, he would sit for hours reading the newest book explaining some abstract aspect of Mississippi's history. He was besotted by history and what it could teach us about humanity and the purpose of life. The books were now dusty because Boyce refused to spend money on a housekeeper. Boyce had more money than he would ever be able to spend, but he was parsimonious in every aspect of his life.

When I arrived in the kitchen, I checked his cabinets to make sure his grocery level was acceptable. Everything appeared to be in order. I gave my regards to everyone. I left his home for my office a few blocks away.

Jackson

MONDAY MORNING, FAULKNER AND I CRAWLED INTO the Jeep. We drove twenty minutes away to Lake Reed, where my family owns a lake house. I have not been to the house in years, and I thought it may be a quiet place to begin my novel. The house was a modest five bedroom brick ranch. It was the place where we spent most of the weekends in the summers of my childhood. There was a huge front porch that covered the entire front of the house because mother thought all southern homes must have large front porches. Six medium columns connected the floor of the porch to the ceiling to support the roof. The front door matched the white color of the shutters and columns

As we pulled into the horse shoe driveway, happy memories of my childhood inundated my mind.

I opened my door, and the smell of fish and lake air rushed through my nostrils. Faulkner jumped out and began marking his new place. We walked around the house and down the back lawn toward the lake. Faulkner immediately jaunted toward the water. He leapt into the air and belly flopped into the water.

Watching him frolic in the water made me jealous. I removed

my shirt, my college ring, my shoes, and laid my wallet on the bank. I dove off the dock. The warm water surrounded me. In that moment, we splashed in the water not caring about the ripples that we caused.

The water was hot for a June morning, yet refreshing. It was calming. I began to float, simply lying in the water and allowed the current to guide my direction. As the water covered my body, Maggie returned to my mind after numerous years of absence. Maggie and I dated in college, and we would secretly escape to the lake house without my parents' knowledge. We would skinny dip in the moon light, and sleep on the screened-in porch at night in the nightly breeze. We loved to lay on the porch and listen the tree frogs as they communicated in the darkness, while watching lightning bugs flicker.

I thought that we would marry, but my family would not allow that to happen. My mother loved Maggie in a southern way. Every southern mother never believes that someone is good enough for her son. With Maggie, mother blatantly advocated for an end of the relationship.

My grandmother was of the same opinion as my mother. Even though Maggie was from a decent family, to Big Momma, Maggie was just a hem above white trash. Her parents' job was not the most important aspect. To Big Momma, Maggie was not a lady. She often questioned me why Maggie was enamored with sports. She could not accept that a lady would throw a football or sit in the grass without a blanket. She insisted that Maggie would bring shame to our family.

There were other reasons for our demise. On some level, we simply grew apart. She wanted children, and I did not. She wanted to live closer to family, and I was adamant about moving away. Those items eventually illuminated other challenges in our relationship and it ended in my junior year at Ole Miss.

Faulkner and I spent several hours of the morning at the dock. Lunch time was calling us indoors.

The absence of people in the house was apparent as I opened the door. Years of dust migrated through the air. I carried the bags from the Jeep and placed them on the kitchen counter. I placed his food in his bowl, and I pulled a sandwich from my bag. I walked throughout the structure and opened all of the windows and turned on lamps. I vowed to have Ms. Sally visit the space soon. I am sure I would use it often over the next year.

I walked into the living room. Floor to ceiling windows replaced the brick walls to the outside in the kitchen and living room. Mother loved cooking dinner or having coffee while being able to stare at the water. I now realized the beauty of it all. I stood in the dusty living room covered in years of absence, staring through the glass watching the peacefulness of the lake. The early summer day was calming. As I stood in the calmness, Faulkner's nails on the hardwood floors startled me back to reality. He was searching the entire house, but he would not go far. He knew that I needed him. We walked through the house. Each room was just as dusty as the others. I am not sure why Sarah Beth had not visited, but it was apparent that no one had entered the house in quite some time.

After lunch, I pulled the laptop from my book bag. I walked to the back porch. The heat attempted to be overbearing, but I travailed and began typing. My mind seemed to catapult words onto the screen. My thoughts became lost in my childhood, of growing up on Magnolia Avenue. I wrote with precision and fury. I wrote for hours. As the afternoon advanced into the early evening, hunger engulfed me.

I decided to drive to a local lake restaurant close by, The Boat Slip, which rests on the bank of the lake. When I arrived there were a few families enjoying dinner. There was no one there that I knew beyond a superficial depth. Lake people were different than district people. I am not sure what made them different; it was just something that we were taught as children. As an adult, I confess that I did see differences among the two citizens of Culpepper. Lake people were more flamboyant about their wealth. I always thought it was funny that lake people would build a million dollar home on land that they rented from the power company.

The host led me to a table on the patio overlooking the water. The sun had just started its descent into the horizon. The beauty of its rays landing softly on the still water enamored me. I loved watching the sunset on the lake. As my second bourbon arrived, Eric and Emily walked onto the restaurant's patio. They were district people who also owned a lake house on rented land. They waved and smiled as they always did, and I responded appropriately.

Eric made his money by purchasing a gas station in the nearby town several years ago. The adventure was profitable, so he began purchasing more, which led Emily to believe she was marrying a large bank account, a way out of her blue collar second marriage.

Indeed, Emily longed to be a member of the social elite. She often expressed at parties in the district the amount of money he and she had spent on a piece of furniture or a piece of art. She loved mentioning who they met at the Magnolia Club.

Antithetically, Eric seemed to be apathetic about climbing the social ladder. To Emily, acquiring social status was her driving force. Although, she would continue trying, she would never be included in the inner social circle of Culpepper because of her past and her lineage. Those things mattered to the people she wanted to become. Pedigree mattered.

As I sat there thinking about Emily and her desire to earn social nobility, I realized how much I hated it. I longed to be normal. The experience with the police officer on the front porch was a reminder of the pain of being a Kensington. Sometimes, I wish I wasn't a Kensington. I wish I had a normal childhood, a normal existence. In Virginia, no one knows who I am or who my family is. No one knows my heritage. To them, I am simply an English professor who struggles with the same challenges of the human condition. When I was at Alabama, I refused to tell people who my father and mother were. I even changed their names on college documents. I was trying to be normal, to be accepted.

When I returned to the lake house, I poured another bourbon and rested in the swing on the screened porch. The repetitious movement calmed my mind. The light at the end of the dock illuminated the shoreline and the edges of the dock. The darkness surrounded me. For a moment, I became Gatsby, staring at the light and my hope.

I sat in the darkness; the lightning bugs communicating to each other. The tree frogs began their courtship. Faulkner lay beside me in the swing. His head rested in my lap. The harmonic chains had already led him to sleep. His breathing was deeper; his paw began swatting into the air. He was dreaming. Perhaps, we both were.

Boyce

I MISS HIM TERRIBLY. HE WAS SO UNDERSTANDING and loving. He rescued me. He was my best friend. Why God? Why did you take him from me? I prayed for you to take me first! Why God?

We travelled everywhere together. When Milk was assassinated in 1978, we travelled to the Castro District to pay our respects. Though the two Mississippi gays could not be open about our love at home, we could in Castro. Castro became our second home. We bought a small condo in the district and every few months, we would leave Culpepper and spend a few days among our people, living together and building a life separate from the hatred of Mississippi and Culpepper. We would often tell others that we were going to Europe, and sometimes we were, but most of the time, we were running naked through the streets of San Francisco. We could be ourselves there.

We went to poetry readings by beatnik poets. We heard Ginsberg read "Howl" to us years after it was published, and in some way it liberated us from our southern lives. Castro became a place of refuge and peace. Though the same hatred of

Mississippi still existed in California at the time, the hatred was more tolerable in the mass populations. We could deal with the hatred because we knew all of our neighbors endured the same hatred. Culpepper was different. We could not endure it. It was just us alone in the district. The hatred would be too overbearing, and our love remained hidden.

We contemplated leaving Culpepper. We could simply move to Castro and live our lives together, but a life separated from family and the district that we loved emerged more important to us both. So, we settled. We settled for second place in each other's lives. Our families and the district was our first love, each other became second.

Second place was not that terrible. We spent almost every night together for 38 years. His house was across the street and three doors down from my house. Culpepper is an old mill town. The founders of the town created a system of underground tunnels that were used to transport supplies from the river to the mills. The river was a block west from the district, and the district is between the river and all of the mills. It was easier to transport the supplies from the docked ships to the basements of the mills for storage and to transport goods for shipment. This was a common arrangement in old manufacturing cities along the river. As time evolved, the tunnels were mostly forgotten and sealed. He and I discovered a tunnel between our houses. We constructed an underground hallway that connected our basements to the tunnel. The tunnel helped shield our relationship for years. It protected us from the hatred. It gave us a love in the darkness of Culpepper.

He knew that I loved him. I knew he loved me. Second place was not that bad.

As I lay here staring into the memories of him, I realize the irony of staying in Culpepper. We stayed because of our families and our friends. I am now here alone, staring into the Monday evening sky watching the sun set. I am here alone staring out the bedroom window. Second place is still not that bad.

Jackson

WHEN I RETURNED FROM THE LAKE TO BRONWYN'S home on Wednesday evening, I decided to explore the artifacts in the attic. I poured a bourbon and walked upstairs. As I walked onto the third floor, I wondered what other family secrets lurked in the boxes. I stepped over the box that I previously left on the floor. I returned to the wall and read the remaining labels. I reached for a box with "Preston" written on the white mailing label, the method Bronwyn chose to organize the memories of our family.

I captured the box and lowered it. I removed the lid and began investigating its contents. There were pictures of me and my siblings at every stage of our childhood. Blake with a bloody nose because he made me angry and my fist gravitated toward his face. Will, as a baby, naked in the kitchen sink as Ms. Sally bathed him. There was a picture of me at three years old riding Skipper, our black lab. The memories reminded me of the good in my childhood. The joys of ignorance and knowledge.

I stood and walked cautiously to the wall of boxes. I browsed for a few minutes, and I found another box label "Boyce." My face crinkled with inquiry. Why did Uncle Bronwyn have a box for the old man across the street? I reached up and carefully lifted the box. As I lifted the lid, I felt a small amount of guilt for rummaging through people's lives, yet I continued my search into his past. The box contained pictures of Boyce and Bronwyn's travels. There were pictures of the two of them holding hands on a beach, a simple caption "Key West, NYE 2000." There were pictures of the two of them sitting in the parlor having martinis. My favorite picture was Boyce playing Bronwyn's piano and Bronwyn was standing behind him with his hands on his shoulders. At the bottom of the piles of pictures were numerous cards that Boyce and given to him. All of them were signed, "With my deepest love, Boyce."

I paused my search. I wanted to talk to Boyce. I ran downstairs, out the door, and across the street. When I reached the opposite sidewalk, I turned left and walked three blocks. Boyce was not on his porch. I rang the bell. Ms. Sally appeared.

Boyce was asleep. This was not the best day for him. He struggled most of the day. He has not eaten all day. Slowly, he was giving up. I retreated to Uncle Bronwyn's attic.

I searched the wall of boxes and found another box labeled "Preston II." It was on the highest shelf. I walked over to the corner to retrieve a stool and methodically climbed atop. Carefully, I lowered the box and myself. I placed the box on the dusty floor. I removed the tape, and glanced inside. I noticed copies of legal documents, copies of deeds, and copies of birth certificates. The original copies were held in our safe deposit box at the bank. I perused the documents out of curiosity. I found certificates of live birth dating back four generations. It was intimidating to read my ancestors' birth statistics. At the bottom of the pile of papers, I read my certificate, Will's certificate, Blake's, and Sarah Beth's. I found a stack of death certificates at the bottom. An old cracking faded brown rubber band held them together.

I lifted the stack and began reading the names of my ancestors and how they left this world. It reminded me of my own mortality. I found Big Daddy's and Big Momma's. I found my father's and Will's certificate. I loved my brother. He taught me so much about life. He was my best friend. I pulled the document from the envelope, and unfolded it, dust rising into the air. It must have been years since someone uncovered the papers. I read. I stopped. I reread. For the box labeled "cause of death" the following words were typed: "Complications due to Acquired Immune Deficiency Syndrome." The word "cancer" was not written anywhere on the document. My heart ached. I sat in the floor aghast and angry. For over a decade, I believed my best friend died of cancer.

On some level, I understood the lie, and I was ashamed.

In that moment, I hated the attic. I hated what it represented. I sat there surrounded by the true history of my family. It was a history that I was not certain that I could handle. My grandfather, my father, my brother, and all of the truths surrounded me.

As I sat there, Faulkner ran up the stairs. He ran to me with his ball in his mouth. He dropped it. I reached for it and tossed it to the far end of the room. He galloped toward it, scooped it up, and ran full speed toward me. He dropped it. He wanted to play. I picked up the ball, and we walked downstairs, through the house, to the median. With each throw, he chased the ball and quickly brought it back to me. He knew in that moment that I needed him.

After a few moments, the old drunk man from before

walked over to us. He did not speak. Faulkner dropped the ball at his feet. In his inebriation, he picked up the ball and flung it; Faulkner ran. For several minutes, they played. He did not care that the man could not throw the ball very far. He did not care that the man's pores emitted alcohol and cigar smoke. He was just happy to have another friend with whom he could play ball. After several minutes, the man picked up the ball. Faulkner jumped with excitement, as he always did knowing the ball was coming. With the ball in his left hand, he raised his right hand in the air over Faulkner's head; his palm was facing the dog. Faulkner immediately stopped jumping around. He sat straight up. His tail stopped moving. The old man gave me the ball, nodded his head, and walked toward First Avenue.

As Faulkner and I continued our game, the sun was lowering itself into the horizon. The purple and pink brush strokes across the sky captured me. The air seemed cooler as the dew slowly fell around us. The noises of the night animals started as Faulkner and I retreated into the house.

Sarah Beth

I WALKED INTO BRONWYN'S HOUSE AND JACKSON WAS
on the phone with Blake, our youngest brother. Blake played
baseball at Ole Miss, and he was drafted to play for the mi-
nors. He now played for Atlanta. Blake was not the smartest
Kensington child. In fact, he was only accepted into Ole Miss
because of legacy; the huge donation to the law school from his
father did not hurt either. As his parents teased him, he barely
had enough sense to come in out of the rain. Though, he was
an excellent athlete; Ole Miss did very well the four years that
Blake was on the team.

As I walked in, Jackson acknowledged me with a grin.

When their conversation ended, Jackson hugged me, and I
followed him into the parlor. He poured us a bourbon. He never
drank during the day; I became apprehensive. I knew something
was wrong.

We sat in the parlor, and he began to tell me that he was
rummaging through more boxes in the attic, when he found a
box that contained Will's death certificate. I reached out to take
it from him. I unfolded it. My mouth dropped.

Jackson also found a box of pictures of our grandfather. As I looked at the pictures, my heart ached. The greatest man in my life was standing over innocent people waiting for the correct moment to touch them with the torch that he held in his right hand. Other pictures depicted Big Daddy dragging men and women off a bus in Jackson. He was kicking a young black man in the head.

The pictures revealed an evil side of Big Daddy, a side that I had never noticed. He was my rock. He was the man who held me through so many difficult times of my childhood.

Jackson held my hand as the tears began to roll carelessly down my cheeks. The most influential man in my life was a racist barbarian. I felt ashamed and angry at the same time. I hated being a Kensington.

When I saw those pictures, I immediately remembered a sorority sister in college who had discovered that her grandfather was in the Klan. When she asked her mother about it, her mother responded, "Those were the days when the Klan was a civic organization. Your grandfather was a good man." I remember her sitting in her dorm room crying, and I was silent and unsure of a response. I simply sat in the quietness. I now know how she felt. I wanted to believe that he was a good man. He was Big Daddy.

Several years ago, I started to create a genealogy record of our family. As I became more entrenched in the process, I discovered numerous facts that I promised to never disclose to my siblings. I discovered papers that bequeathed slaves from fathers to sons and from fathers to wives. Those papers jolted my soul. I am southern, but I did not expect that from my family. I did not expect my grandfather could do those horrible things.

I took a sip of the bourbon. As he held my hand and with the tears still falling, I sat silent, just as I did in my dorm room many years ago. To be honest, I did not know what to say. Big Daddy was everything that I loved about our family. When I was in junior high, I was riding my bike and a car hit me. My left leg was broken, and I had three cracked ribs. I was covered in scratches from the red bricks of the street. For days, he came into my room and brought me ice cream. He told me he hid it from my parents and Ms. Sally. He promised the coldness would help heal my bones. When I married Gavin, I asked Big Daddy and my father both to walk me down the aisle. He was my rock.

The bourbon did nothing for the numbness. I asked Jackson to walk me home.

Joshua

MOMMY AND UNCLE JACKSON WALKED ACROSS THE grass. I could tell she was crying. Uncle Jackson made her cry. Why did he do that? She must have done something bad. Uncle Jackson is my favorite uncle. He is a nice uncle. He gives me chocolate. I ran to them. I hugged mommy. I asked why she was crying and what did Uncle Jackson do to her. They both laughed. I knew it was not Uncle Jackson. I like it when they laugh. I ran to the swing. The grass tickled my feet. I loved running through the grass barefoot. This time, I crawled up on top of it. "Push me Uncle Jackson. Push me." The tire swing was now my horse. He was running through the grass. He was running as fast as he could through the grass. My horse was running, and I couldn't stop it. I couldn't stop the running horse.

Jackson

SARAH BETH AND I SAT IN THE PARLOR, BOTH STAR-
ing at the reality of the sins of our father. He was a Supreme
Court Judge when Will died, and I know that his political connections would be severed should anyone find out that his eldest son died of AIDS. This made me hate him even more. He
ripped Will's ability to die in truth away from him. Every headline across Mississippi read, "Supreme Court Judge Loses His
Son to Cancer." The governor spoke at Will's funeral. It could
have been a powerful time to address the stigma of the disease.
My father stole that moment from him.

Sarah Beth hugged me, and I grabbed a bag from the parlor before walking her home. After walking her, I walked to
Boyce's house. He needed me. I brought a new pair of hair
clippers that I had purchased for this purpose and a smaller
trimmer. I walked up the steps. He was sitting in his regular
position on the porch; his walker was close. Today was obviously a good day for him. He smiled and asked how I was. I
responded wittingly and deliberately. The new knowledge of
him and my uncle resonated on my psyche. I wanted to discuss

their relationship, and I was hoping the correct moment would surface soon.

I helped him enter the house. I did not want the neighbors to be aware of what I was doing. He sat in an old Queen Anne dining chair in the dining room. It was a beautiful room, with one wall dedicated to housing his family's crystal. His house was inundated with antiques from all over the world. He was a devout collector of old things. I placed a towel around his neck before the doorbell rang.

I walked to the door. Auden and Victoria offered salutations, and we returned to the dining room. Boyce made a few inappropriate comments about Victoria's apparel. Teasing Victoria was an entertaining event for Boyce, another indication that he was having a good day. I placed the black guard on the clippers. I began cutting his hair.

"Okay, Dr. Kensington, I hope you cut hair better than you teach."

"Boyce, I have clippers. Do you want to keep your ear?"

He and I had developed a relationship premised on teasing each other, as well. We would often spar with witty comments that playfully degraded each other. Boyce was incredibly intelligent. His vocabulary far exceeded my own, though I would never allow him to know that fact.

As Boyce and I were sparing, Auden picked up the daily newspaper. "Did ya'll see where Justice Hardaway was murdered?" Auden asked.

"According to the paper, it was his ex-wife. It was a quick death," Victoria replied.

"Or was it the machine?" Boyce inquired.

We all laughed at his humor. At Ole Miss, there is an urban

legend that the machine, a sub-group within the Greek system, controlled the university and the state. It was rumored that a president of the university was fired because he made the machine angry. According to the rumor, the group graduated and continued controlling the state through secretive channels. Everyone who goes to Ole Miss has blamed the machine on something in his or her life. It was nice that Boyce's mind was not weakening; he too chuckled reminiscing his college days.

I enjoyed spending time with Auden and Victoria, but I secretly wished they would leave. I wanted to discuss Boyce's relationship with my uncle. Auden made martinis for the three of us. I sipped as I cut his hair. When I had completed his hair, I used the smaller trimmer on the more delicate areas on his face.

After a few martinis, the Harrington's decided to retrieve their dinner. I chose to stay with Boyce a few more minutes. As we sat there, the silence was unbearable.

"Boyce, how well did you know my uncle?"

At the mention of my uncle, his eyes flooded with tears. The fluid was overwhelming. They poured down his cheeks. A sense of remorsefulness covered me because my selfishness had caused Boyce pain.

"Jackson, your uncle was my best friend for nearly forty years. We travelled everywhere together. We laughed and cried together. I miss him more than you will ever know. He was my confidant. He was the Jonathan to my David."

He began to tell me stories of their travels over Europe and South America. They were detained and later released in Amsterdam. His stories were mesmerizing. He loved my uncle. Yet, he never once mentioned the words. He never once mentioned a loving relationship. Publicly, they were best friends, and even with me, Boyce desired to maintain those appearances. I chose not tell him that my uncle had kept every card and love letter that he sent to him. I wanted Boyce to die with dignity and grace, and the appearances that he desired.

After I helped Boyce to bed, I walked through his front door, as Aubrey walked up the steps. Even at the end of the day, she was incredibly polished and poised.

"Good Evening Jackson. How are you?"

"I am great. Boyce is in bed."

"I came to check on him. But, now you and I are going to have a drink."

As we walked down the sidewalk, Aubrey guided my eyes to each neighbor's house. As she did, she disclosed information. We walked by Eric and Emily's home. I was informed that Emily loved to name drop and pretend that she was born with a silver spoon. A few weeks ago, Eric became so inebriated that he shared with Aubrey their true financial situation. According to Eric, if three of his gas stations did not meet their financial goals for three consecutive months, they would lose everything. He fretted an economic breakdown in our country. Eric had grown his company too quickly because he needed money to help Emily increase her social mobility.

We continued down the street. Cara was a plain divorced middle aged woman with one son in a prestigious private college in Alabama. As we passed, a young military officer walked out of her front door. I glanced questioningly at Aubrey, who informed me that Cara loved the young, white army officers.

Two houses down from Cara were the Hardings, a physician and a mother who worked from home raising two children. At times, he would enjoy too much whiskey and released his inebriation verbally on his wife. She would threaten to leave him, but his money was stronger than his words or her pain. She was a nurse that Dr. Harding courted while he was married. Until she became pregnant, he had no desire to rear children or be with her for an extended period. Dr. Harding's wife discovered the affair, and he purchased a home in the historic district for his new wife.

Across the street were Grace and Sawyer Huntington, a couple who traveled around the world. They loved great food and great bourbon. Grace's family owned a mill, and Sawyer, a physician, was from a long tradition of physicians. Both family names were Culpepper founders.

As we talked, Whit was dancing in the median.

Aubrey gave me a plethora of information about the neighbors of the historic district. I was listening to her intently because the information would become useful to me.

We continued our walk to the commercial area of Magnolia. The sun had completely reached the horizon. As we stepped out of the historic district, Aubrey pointed to an older man urinating in the bushes. Mack was 85 years old and had more money than God. He owned property all over the south, mostly near a body of water. It was rumored that he had committed numerous felonies, but was never convicted. He smuggled drugs over the Mexican border on a regular basis. Mack was known to pay multiple women simultaneously to help him enjoy his life to the fullest, even in his aging state. Although, his mobility was hindered by painful knees, he endured the pain for an evening walk around his block a few nights a week. When he completed his task, he waved and slowly meandered south on Magnolia to his enormous estate that he bought three years ago from the Lexingtons, who moved to Naples to enjoy their retirement from the mill business.

As we walked into the restaurant, I noticed Sarah Beth and Gavin sitting at a table. I excused myself for a few moments and walked over to them. I hugged them both. I invited Sarah Beth to lunch the next day.

Aubrey and I sat at the bar for a few hours laughing. I loved how southern she was. Her long deep accent was proof she was from another part of the state. I loved the way she could turn a one syllable word into three syllables. She always dressed as if she belonged in a Southern Living magazine.

We sat at the bar, and she continued to share with me secrets of the neighborhood.

Whit

I AM IN THE GRASS. YOU ARE IN THE STREET. I WILL come close to you if you ask me to and bring you to the grass. I am safe from traffic. I can make you safe. You are on hard clay. Does that hurt your feet? Hello, I am talking to you. Hey, you standing right there. Does the clay hurt your feet? The hard things that seem to go on and on and on down the street. The clump. The clack. The clump. The clack. The red hard clay. Because the grass feels great to my feet. I took off my shoes. I am running barefoot in the soft grass. Hello, you over there. I know you hear me. I am calling to you. Listen to my words. I can help you. Just ask me. I can help you find the soft grass.

Jackson

AUBREY WAS A BEAUTIFUL WOMAN. SHE SEEMED TO know everyone in the district and about all of their lives. As we traveled north on Magnolia, I listened intently. These families were relatively new to the district since my departure. I was unaware of most of their lives. I have not visited the district for years, and prior to that I rarely came home. I had a wonderful time with her last night.

When I woke this morning, I completed the same routine that I have done every morning for the past few years. I am not sure why I find peace in them, but I do. As I was on my morning run, I began contemplating the novel, the purpose of my return to Culpepper. As my shoes hit the red bricks, the music from my phone energized me more and more. I ran faster this morning than I have in a long time. I ran without a goal in mind, rather I ran aimlessly through the district. I turned left down a street and a block later, I was standing beside the river. The smell of fish diffused into the air. I turned left and ran along the river on the dirty sidewalk. The river was high on this early morning. The geese walked carelessly on the banks. A group of young men

floated on paddle boards in the middle of the river. They allowed
the current to guide them slowly to the south. The birds sang to
each other. Squirrels ran sporadically from the river's edge to the
sidewalk. I ran, lost in the calmness of my surroundings. I ran,
lost in myself for quite some time.

I desired to write. I ran while writing in my mind, allowing
the run to write for me. The run became the striking of the keys,
concerted and hard. I wrote.

I could feel the language within me calling out for freedom.
It longed to be the truth on the pages. I wrote lost in the equanimity of nature. As a child, I ran down this same path. It was
the path that protected our hop scotch squares, drawn in layers
of chalk and erasable by the summer rains. As I aged, a football
replaced the squares. I ran down the path to catch the ball that
my father threw. I cradled the ball with pride because he was
proud of me. I was his son.

With every step, the memories rose from the path under me
and grabbed me. They embraced my soul. Those were the good
memories of a forgotten childhood.

When I returned to Uncle Bronwyn's, I ran upstairs to
the master bedroom and pulled my laptop from my bag. I was
sweaty. My body covered with the words that would soon pop-
ulate the screen. I sat on the bed. I opened the laptop. I began
typing; the words became sentences. I smiled. At some point
during the morning, the doorbell rang. I ignored it, consumed in
the construction of a family in a small southern town.

In the evening hours, I decided dinner was necessary. I closed
the laptop, and as I stood, my body was hesitant. The hours of
sitting on the bed typing was hindering me. Slowly, I made
it to the door. I realized that I had been in the same position

for hours, writing. It was time for dinner. The smell of my run from this morning became apparent. I showered, redressed, and walked north on Magnolia.

I walked into The Cellar, a new restaurant in the commercial part of Magnolia. I spoke softly to the hostess and made my way to the bar. As I sat down, I noticed neighbors walking toward me to exchange salutations. I stood. We spoke briefly, and I returned to my seat. Matt, the bartender, placed a Hillrock Bourbon on the rocks in front of me. Its light amber color kissed my lips with a slight cold tingle. As I examined the dinner menu, I noticed a tall blonde woman walk through the door. She was stunningly gorgeous. There were two seats remaining at the bar, one on each side of me.

She sat to my left. I ordered the pork tenderloin and returned the menu to Matt. I sipped slowly. She glanced over at me and asked, "What type of bourbon?"

"Hillrock."

"Nice. An upstate New York solera aged bourbon. Great choice."

Her knowledge surprised me, "Yes. It's great. Not many people know of it."

"I'm a fan of a great bourbon."

"So am I," I replied.

She ordered a Hillrock, and we began casual chatting. She had just arrived in town to open a new national bank branch in Culpepper. She was staying at a local hotel until she found a place to rent. I offered her the names of some local property owners who may have a rental available. She was currently living in Charleston, a town that she truly hated to leave, which I understood.

89

Our food was served, and we continued enjoying the bourbon. We laughed, and she laughed at my childhood growing up in Culpepper.

She was beautiful. Her long naturally blonde hair ended at her shoulders, and every few moments she used her index finger to place a few blonde strands behind her ear. Her light blue eyes were the focal point of her tanned face. We chatted for a couple of hours while we enjoyed dinner. I gave Matt my card for our meals. After she thanked me, I asked for her phone. Surprisingly, she handed it to me after entering the code to unlock it. I sent myself a text. She smiled.

I walked her to her car, and then I turned left on Magnolia to walk home.

It was dark now. The air was cooler. The street lights guided my path. As I walked past my family home, I stopped and looked at the place where Big Daddy had lived and raised his family. It was the same place that my father had raised his family. It was dark both inside and outside. I walked up the driveway around the house to the backyard. I walked toward the old iron swing. I sat in the swing and floated through the air. The only visible light was in the cottage, Ms. Sally's home. I sat there floating back and forth in the swing staring at that light. A clap of thunder radiated the darkness. The sky illuminated, and the pounding rain began. Yet, I sat in the swing floating back and forth. The rain covering me and ricocheting off the metal swing. As I floated in the darkness, the rain soaked my skin. I stared at the light from the cottage.

Corbin

"PHOEBE, IT HAS BEEN A GREAT FEW MONTHS. BUT, I do not think we should see each other anymore. I am sorry. I just don't think we are right for each other. I wish you the best of luck." Sent. I walked as quickly as I could. I needed to be at Aubrey's before 2:00. She has a baby shower to go to at 3:00. I enjoyed Aubrey, more so than Phoebe. I also needed to go into the office today to work on a case. My uncle can be an asshole sometimes.

Auden Harrington was one of the best defense attorneys in the state. He was an Ole Miss grad and lost few cases. His wife was also an attorney, but she avoided a public institution for a much better and exclusive school, Vanderbilt. Victoria was one of the brightest women that I knew. She had practiced law for a number of years, and was one of Auden's losses, which he still bemoans to this day. Victoria was now the Chief Judge for the Fifth Circuit of United States District Court. Both individuals were incredibly respected in the state of Mississippi.

I graduated from Tulane's law school two years ago, and my uncle offered me a job in his firm. It is a well-respected firm with offices around the state. I loved the law, and how the manipulation of the meaning of the law could provide such an adrenaline rush.

Auden and Victoria were married several years ago. They dated for ten years before the two married because both were career focused. One morning, Auden chartered a plane and flew twenty of their closest acquaintances to Martha's Vineyard for Victoria's birthday. When the plane landed, everyone took separate cars to the same hotel where Auden had rented their rooms. When Auden and Victoria walked into the hotel's penthouse suite, Victoria walked over to a wall of windows that provided a view of the exquisite gardens. In one of the gardens, there were twenty perfectly placed white chairs, ten on each side of an aisle, only a beautiful white carpet runner separating the two sides. The outer perimeter was constructed with large white lattice walls that were stuffed with huge white Lilies.

Victoria remarked about the beauty of the wedding venue. She turned around and Auden had placed a dress on the bed. It was the same dress that Victoria commented about while in Paris three months ago. It was an elegant white gown. Tears rolled down her cheeks. Auden took her into his arms and gently kissed her. He stepped back and while holding her hands, he knelt and asked Victoria to spend the rest of her life with him.

The wedding was held that evening, with a reception in the hotel's ballroom. It was an elaborate event. They stayed at Martha's Vineyard for the weekend. On the following Tuesday, the Harringtons left for Rome on their honeymoon.

I see the love between my uncle and aunt. They continually chastise me for not settling down. They worry that I will forever roam the world, sewing my wild oats. I had my heart broken in college. I met a fantastic girl in a bar. Molly was amazing, and I slowly began falling in love with her, while she was not falling in love with me. When I discovered her with another man, I was angry. The advice my aunt gave me was that I can't shake a whore tree and expect a virgin to fall down. She believed that the respectable wife can only be found in church, the Junior League, or some other aristocratic function. It was 1:45. I walked up Aubrey's steps two at a time, looking to raise the number.

Sarah Beth

JOSHUA LOVES SIMPLY LAYING IN THE GRASS. I LOVE his innocence. When he was born, the umbilical cord was wrapped around his neck. The doctor performed an emergency Cesarean Section. Too, I almost died. When Joshua was able to take his first breath, the doctors could not evaluate how much damage the lack of oxygen had caused him. After a few months, we began to notice some minor effects, but it wasn't until he began learning language that the full extent of the constriction became apparent. He will always be locked in the mind of an innocent child, protected from the realities of life.

As he sat in the grass, Julia came over to play with him. As the game of tag began, I noticed Corbin leaving Aubrey's a few houses north of mine. Honestly, I am not sure why they believe that no one knows what is really happening with those two. We all know, and most of us have gossiped about it. She is almost double his age. I wonder if Auden and Victoria know.

Jackson just ran by us. He waved. When he graduated from high school, Jackson basically moved away from the district. He came home occasionally, but even during the summers he found an internship or a reason to not permanently return home. I am not sure why he is staying in Uncle Bronwyn's house and not our parents' house. It was odd to me.

When he announced that he was going into a PhD program, my father almost disowned him. Father expected him to go to law school at Ole Miss. His disappointment was felt by everyone for several weeks. Jackson entered Alabama with a full assistantship, which was good because Preston would never pay for his non-law school choice. When he graduated, we all visited Tuscaloosa, and watched his doctoral advisor raise the dark blue velvet hood over his head and lowered it slowly around his neck. It was a beautiful ceremony welcoming Jackson into the academy. He was offered several faculty positions, one at Ole Miss, but he chose a small private liberal arts college in Virginia.

Father was again disappointed and angry that Jackson chose to live four states away. He rarely came home, in fact, he only returned during the important holidays, Thanksgiving and Christmas. When he did come home, he chose to stay with Uncle Bronwyn. He said because he thought he was lonely. Though he didn't come home often, he did speak to mother almost daily on the phone. I rarely heard anyone mention him speaking to our father. We talked weekly, and he and Blake were always close, even as kids.

Being a kid in the Kensington house was difficult at times. Blake thought he was the favorite. He was the baseball star, like our father. Blake could murder us all and as long as he could still pitch, our father would defend him in court. But, in high school, he moved in with Uncle Bronwyn, which I never understood the reason. It was something that we simple did not question, and we never spoke of it. Jackson was the real favorite and the smart

95

kid. Because he was the intellectual, our father believed that he would be an excellent attorney who would eventually lead his firm. Will was the perfect child who always behaved. I felt like the outsider. I didn't play sports, and I was not smart enough. I existed through my childhood.

I discovered who I was at Agnes Scott, where my college experience helped shape me. When I entered the Peace Corps, I was able to really understand my own humanity and purpose. It's also where I met Gavin.

As I sat in the grass watching the children play, three police cars raced by us, their loud sirens blaring through the air. I stood to watch them travel down First Avenue. Two black Suburbans with tinted windows followed. I watched as all five cars stopped at the Winchester's house, five houses from me.

I told Julia to take Joshua inside. The noise had summoned several neighbors from their doors; Aubrey was one of those neighbors. I waved to her, and we met on the sidewalk in front of my house. We stood and watched a few minutes before joining a mob of neighbors who decided to walk cautiously and curiously to the Winchester's house.

The house was surrounded by the police officers. Suddenly, an officer walked Stanford and Vivian Winchester through the front door. Both of my neighbors were in handcuffs.

Phoebe

AS I OPENED THE DOOR, I COULD FEEL THE HUMID summer air as it slapped my body. I walked out to retrieve the morning paper. I glanced to my left, and I noticed Jackson standing on the porch. He was wearing running shorts without a shirt. He was stretching. He waved and smiled. I responded appropriately. As I turned to walk into the house, Jackson walked over to speak with me.

He asked if I wanted to grab a drink one evening this week. He wanted to chat about the neighborhood. I agreed. He smiled and began running north on Magnolia.

I hoped he did not intend our drink to be a date. He is an incredibly nice guy, but I am not sure about dating anyone. Victoria introduced me to a nice physician, but I noticed small annoying character flaws, or that is what I told everyone. The truth is that he was not Sam. I missed Sam. I am still so mad at God for taking my husband. He could have let him live. Sam was a good man, a great husband. We had a small child. God just ripped that from my life. Victoria's friend was not Sam. Jackson is not Sam.

Sam and I met when I was in my early twenties. He was an army officer who came to Culpepper to go to school on post. He was attractive and smart. We began dating, and we married after a year. For a few years, we travelled the world because he was often deployed. When our child was born, he decided to leave the army and become a police officer. He loved protecting people. He loved protecting me. It seems like yesterday that he was here with me.

I unfolded the paper and the front page headline read, "IRS Confiscates Local Couple's Computers, Freezes Accounts, and Charges Fraud and Tax Evasion." As I read the article, I was shocked. Stanford and Vivian Winchester, a prominent couple in Culpepper, were charged with fraud and tax evasion through real estate transactions. According to the article, the local couple, who owned numerous rental properties in Culpepper, purchased property through two payments. In public documents, the owner would sell the house under market value, and the Winchesters would give a second check to the owner, which was not listed in the closing documents. Thus, their sells were impacting property taxes. Also, the owner would not disclose the second check to the IRS for tax purposes.

I knew Stan and Vivi well. They were well respected citizens of the historic district and the city. I was saddened by this news. Now, I realized why the black Suburbans were racing down First Avenue toward their house the other day.

I sipped my coffee. I didn't really miss Corbin. On page three, the headline read, "Klan March Scheduled in Culpepper on Saturday."

I glanced up from my paper to see Whit. He was drunker than Cooter Brown, and it was only the morning. He was walking through the median staggering from side to side. His long brown hair pulled back in a ponytail. He wore brown slacks and a button up, which was his normal attire. He stopped and began talking to a squirrel. I chuckled aloud and returned to the morning news.

Jackson

IT WAS A HOT HUMID MORNING, BUT I NEEDED TO clear my head from a night of writing. I needed a great run this morning. I enjoyed writing in the evening with a bourbon. Last night, I wrote late into the night. The words flew from my mind, drawn to the white blank screen. Quickly, words became phrases, and phrases became sentences, filling screens of pages. I wrote furiously. The bourbon freeing the constraints of my mind. Words from the past and words of the future coalesced together on the screen.

I ran quickly. I reached Boyce's house. He was not sitting outside on the porch. In fact, I have not seen him on his porch in a few mornings. When I take lunch and dinner to him, he is in his bedroom lying in bed watching television. I stopped and ran up his porch steps. I reached up and located the key that he kept outside on the door frame. I inserted the key and turned the knob.

Boyce was in his bed lying there. His breathing was shallow. I touched his wrist. He opened his eyes. I sat on his bed beside him. He smiled as I asked how he was feeling. He said he was tired and simply wanted to sleep. I told him I would return at lunch.

A few months ago, Boyce fell and has never completely recovered. To me, he appeared to be declining. My heart ached for him, but I was also happy that he would be with Bronwyn soon.

I walked out the front door and returned the key to its hidden spot.

I continued running north on Magnolia. Cara was entering her car, preparing to begin her workday. Victoria was leaving for work. She stopped me and made arrangements for dinner this week. Aubrey was walking home from a breakfast appointment. She waved and smiled. The humidity was thick and wet on my skin.

I turned right on 11th Street toward First Avenue, where I turned right, traveling south on First. I ran by Aubrey's house. It was an exquisite smaller home with four square columns as the focal point of the porch. There was a balcony on the second floor that overlooked the front yard. Aubrey attended Ole Miss, for this reason, an Ole Miss Flag rested on the second column, while an American flag rested on the third column.

I ran past Sarah Beth's home. Joshua was in the yard playing with their black lab. Brick was incredibly patient with Joshua. They were best friends.

I continued to First Avenue where I turned right toward Magnolia. To my left was a large public park which contained a large statue of Robert E. Lee at the entrance. It had been in this park all of my life. Until now, it never taunted me. What it represented caused the photographs to resurface in my mind. I hated Big Daddy as much as I hated my father. I hated being a Kensington.

101

I glanced and noticed Mack was having a conversation with a man who appeared to be homeless. My curiosity drew me from the anger, and I watched from afar. Mack reached into his pocket and counted several bills, which he handed to the man. The man hugged Mack, who returned the gesture. Mack turned to his left and walked over to a magnolia tree where began relieving himself onto the tree's trunk. I returned to my run.

I decided to run through the park. As I ran down the sidewalk, Mack called and motioned for me to come toward him. It was awkward, and I wanted to continue in the opposite direction. At first, I pretended to not hear him. But, he became persistent, and I ran to him. He was zipping his pants, and he reached his hand out to shake mine. I reached to remove my earbuds in my ears, holding one in each ear to avoid shaking his hand.

He was in his eighties with a full gray beard and long hair. He wore small glasses, although today he was wearing a black eye patch over his right eye. Mack was loquacious. I wanted to place the earbuds back in and run away, but my southern upbringing would not allow that to happen. He seemed to ramble on and on about his life in Hollywood and all of the women that he had bedded. On a few occasions, he repositioned himself because of his knee. It was obvious that he was in pain. After a few moments, I noticed a woman was walking across the opposite end of the park. He continued talking without noticing her. She walked up and spoke to him. It was obvious that they knew each other. She asked if I was going to join them. Mack glanced at me, smiled, and jokingly said I wasn't his type. I nodded my head and placed the earbuds in as I ran away.

I continued my run through the park. I ran past the Confederate statues with homeless individuals sleeping beneath them;

the summer heat had not awakened them. I do not remember seeing people who were homeless when I was growing up. We played football and soccer under these statues. I ran by an oak tree and stopped. I walked over to it. Still carved in the trunk was my name and my first high school girlfriend. I laughed. I had forgotten how child-like I was. I reached and touched the carving. My fingers caressed the indentation of the heart that separated my name from Mary Beth's name. I immediately wondered what happened to her.

I continued my run through the park. The lawns were inundated with magnolia trees. I noticed a playground where several children were climbing or swinging. Their parents were huddled together drinking their coffee and laughing. I waved as I ran by the parents.

The temperature was rising quickly. As I exited the park, I realized that I was on Fourth Avenue, where the old mills were once located. Most of which have been refurbished into expensive lofts. At one time, Culpepper was one of the wealthiest zip codes in the nation. There were more cotton mills in this area than any other part of the southeast. It was a thriving industrial area.

I turned and continued toward Magnolia. I was lost in the moment. The busy cars, the people buzzing to work, the normalcy of life was absent from me. I ran finding solace in the experience and in the thumping of my feet on the pavement. I felt free for the first time in a long time. I simply ran into the freedom.

The sweat began amplifying the rays of the sun. I could feel the slight sting of the sun on my skin. It reminded me of my humanity. The sounds from the church's bell tower awakened me. I found myself on Second Avenue across from First Baptist.

The bells called for me. I was drawn to them. I walked across the street toward the massive doors. Without pausing, I reached for the handle, opened the door, and walked into the vestibule. The doors to the sanctuary were open. The lights were extinguished. The sun rays through the stained glass windows guided my steps to the back pew. I was wet from the sweat of my run. I was shirtless, and my body was covered in the stench of my daily routine. I sat on the pew staring into the darkness surrounding the pulpit and choir loft. My eyes turned to the right. I saw Christ hanging naked on the cross depicted in the glass. The two others crucified on each side of him. I sat in the stillness dirty on the back pew.

Joshua

I LOVE YOU, BRICK. HE LIKES TO LICK MY FACE WHEN I am sitting in the grass. Brick, there is Uncle Jackson. See him? He's running, but I don't see anything chasing him. Running. Chasing. Brick get the ball. Get the ball, Brick. Brick, get the ball. Don't lick my face. Ball, Brick, Ball. Uncle Jackson is running again.

Victoria

AS I DID EVERY MORNING BEFORE WORK, I DROVE TO Boyce's to make sure his needs were met. When I arrived this morning, he was still in bed. He seemed morose. He yelled obscenities at me for disturbing his sleep. I told him I loved him, and left him under his quilt.

Boyce was an angry man sometimes, but I loved him. I bought his groceries and paid his house bills. I had power of attorney for his affairs. He trusted me. One time, he screamed at me for not driving to Big Lots ten miles away to purchase a cleaner because it was fifty cents cheaper. I know he cares for me. He's not the same Boyce from years ago. A few years ago, he turned into an angry man who seemed not to care about others' feelings. Often, I questioned what caused his personality change. He simply walked away from the conversation.

As he lay in his bed, I longed for the old Boyce, the one who loved musicals and martinis. The man who was filled with intellectualism and pomposity. I missed the way that his fingers glided over the piano keys, playing rifts that seemed to appear from his mind so easily. He was so talented, yet he simply stopped playing around the commencement of his anger.

When I arrived at my office, I phoned Sally and asked her to check on Boyce throughout the day. I walked over to my office window and opened the blinds. My office was on First Avenue, two blocks from my house. As I glanced out of the windows, I saw Jackson. He was running. I am glad that he came home for his sabbatical. I have not seen him since Bronwyn's funeral. He rarely came home when his parents were alive.

Elizabeth was a dear friend of mine. I miss her tremendously. She was incredibly involved in Culpepper and Mississippi. There were few prominent organizations in the state that she had not served on their board of directors, but her favorite was the Mississippi Museum of Art in Jackson. She was an art history major in college and was an avid art collector. She has purchased seven Haffners, including the original "The Banshee and Her Conspiracy." Elizabeth adored Bo Bartlett and his work, owning ten of his originals. She had Pound paint her family portraits, which were astounding. Several years ago she began purchasing sculptures after viewing Hunt Rettig's work. She owned an extensive collection, and often loaned part of her collection to museums around the south. Elizabeth was also a wonderful philanthropist, which she proved by giving her time and her money.

She was standing in the kitchen when her heart simply stopped. She was in wonderful health. She fell face forward onto the kitchen floor, and Ms. Sally walked in and found her. She rests in the cemetery at First Baptist. Her funeral was one of the largest ones that I have witnessed at that church. It was standing room only and overflowed into the front lawn.

I will never forget the eulogy that Jackson offered at her funeral. He sat on the front pew between Sarah Beth and Ms. Sally with the rest of his family. Although I was a few pews behind him, I could hear his mourning. He lost the most important person in his life. As the pastor called him to the pulpit, the tears miraculously suspended. He was dressed perfectly in a black suit with a black tie because he understood the necessity of formality. He stood behind the pulpit and spoke of the most influential woman in his life.

He referenced the life of Ruth and her unwavering faith and loyalty. The words he shared about his mother's faith rose from a broken spirit.

I know he felt guilty for leaving her alone. Although they spoke frequently on the phone, he rarely came home. His guilt was physically apparent as he spoke that day.

I stared out the window, watching Jackson run. He looked just like his mother. She loved him dearly. She was so proud of his accomplishments. He had published several books, and she bought each book for all of her friends. I own all of them. His second one was on the New York Times best sellers list. Elizabeth told me one time Jackson was offered a job at Princeton, but he refused it because of the cold and snow. We laughed because that was the child we knew growing up. He was always a practical child, who believed in the basic tenets of right and wrong. There was not a lot of gray space in his life. His mother and I worried about him. He was a special kid who needed a special person to deal with his intellectualism.

I missed his mother and her ability to make me feel loved. When I was having a horrible day, she made me feel as if I was the Queen of England. She cared about her friends. Her life could be falling apart and she would still ask about me and how I was doing and genuinely care about my response. Seeing him reminded me of how badly I missed my friend.

A light knocking at my door summoned my attention. The door opened, "Judge Harrington, Aubrey is here to see you."

Jackson

I WENT TO BOYCE'S HOUSE EVERY DAY THIS WEEK TO visit with him. He had only four visitors: me, the Harringtons, and Aubrey. The other neighbors never visited. The neighborhood had detached itself from him. He lay alone in the house that once was the epicenter of the district's social affairs. His home was the place for countless gatherings and entertainment. He welcomed his neighbors into his home, even the ones of whom he was not incredibly fond. In his last days, they all abandoned him when he was unusable.

Now, he remained in bed all week. He would not rise to eat lunch or dinner. He was weaker. His breathing worsened. The physician visited, and instructed us to coax Boyce out of bed. He would not survive much longer simply lying in the bed. He must begin eating again. Victoria hired Ms. Sally to stay with him throughout the nights.

His body was slowly decaying, and his soul cried desperately for his creator and his friend.

Although he was much older than I was, his sickness and separation became more real to me. There were times that I stared at his frail failing body knowing that part of his illness was his lack of a desire to live. He needed Bronwyn. His anger about the loss of Bronwyn inundated every part of his life. His anger chased his friends and family away. He had nothing for which to live. He desired death, and he lay in the bed reaching for a hope in the unknown.

In many ways, it was depressing. Boyce had lived an amazing life, surrounded by friends and family. He lived a very privileged life, one where money really was not an issue. He travelled around the world. He loved someone for over forty years, someone who loved him in return. Now, his body lay nearly lifeless in the bed alone. He was simply alone.

Aubrey

I SAT BESIDE BOYCE ON HIS BED. I CARESSED HIS LEFT hand in my hands. The syringe lay lifeless and empty in my purse. I prayed. I prayed harder than I have ever prayed before, praying for him and for me. I hoped God was listening to my words. Tears flowed down my cheeks. His breath stopped, which caused more tears. I dropped to my knees beside his bed. I prayed harder. I wanted to release my feelings into the air, knowing I gave him his desire. He was free. Simply free.

Jackson

THE MORNING BEGAN AS A BEAUTIFUL SUNNY SATUR-
day in Culpepper. I was on mile four running south on Magnolia when a loud clap of thunder reverberated through the sky. It
startled me. As quickly as the noise appeared, huge droplets of
rain began falling. I glanced to my left and realized I was in front
of Boyce's house. I ran quickly up the steps. I love hard rains
when the sky was so blue and sunny. Suddenly, the rain stopped
as quickly as it started. I stepped off the porch onto the sidewalk.
Aubrey appeared on the porch with tears filling her eyes.

I reached to hug her. She shook her head and walked toward
her car parked on the street.

In that moment, I realized that Boyce had died.

Victoria parked her car in the place that Aubrey vacated. She
walked up and took my hand. Tears were forming in her eyes. She
loved him. Together we walked into his house. We walked through
the parlor and turned left, moving beyond the grand piano. We
entered his bedroom. His lifeless body lay peacefully in his bed. The
covers were pulled to his chin, and his eyes were forced closed. He
seemed so perfect in his stillness. His body was still warm.

Victoria reached over and started to make the room appear more appropriate for the coroner and whoever else may enter. She walked around the room and collected any items on the floor. She fluffed the pillows on the sofa in his room. She turned the television off. She opened the blinds. The room was the perfect place for his departure.

As I watched her, I realized the depth of her love for him. Boyce was a true southerner. He cared so deeply for appropriate appearances. Throughout his life, he maintained an appearance that was predicated on others' perceptions. As Victoria cleaned his bedroom, she was showing Boyce how much she loved him, even in his death.

The doorbell sounded. Victoria nodded, which gave me permission to open the door.

The ambulance stopped silently in front of Boyce's home. People entered the house, and Victoria led them to his bedroom. She walked into the library. I followed her, and I closed the door behind me. Her tears were more profound. Each droplet released her anger. She was angry that Boyce simply stopped fighting. She was angry that Boyce gave up. She tightened her fists and shook them into the air. She was hurting. There was a slight knock on the door. I slowly opened it. Auden walked into the room toward her. He held her as she cried. I walked out, pulling the door shut behind me. As I walked away, I heard her sadness through the door.

Cara

I WALKED INTO FIRST BAPTIST A FEW MINUTES BE-
fore the service began. As I pulled the huge mahogany door and
entered into the sanctuary, the emptiness of the room drowned
me. I walked to the front of the church to rest my eyes one final
time on my neighbor. Victoria had placed several photographs
and an oil portrait of Boyce on a table that was placed to the
right of the altar. I did not pass thirty people in total as I walked.
I stood over Boyce's urn and smiled at my friend. He was finally
at peace. I touched the urn and said goodbye.

I turned to walk to an appropriate pew. Most of the people
in the church were not historic district citizens. Auden and Victoria sat with Jackson on the right side of the church near the
middle. Phoebe was sitting in the back right corner of the room.
I sat in the back, on the opposite end of Phoebe's pew. Aubrey
walked by me, and as she passed, she touched my shoulder to
acknowledge me. I did not see Eric and Emily, the Winchesters,
nor Dr. Harding and his wife. Sarah Beth and Gavin walked in
solemnly. They sat beside Jackson and the Harringtons.

Dr. Michael Kennedy, the pastor of First Baptist, walked to

the pulpit. He welcomed everyone into the church, even though it was a sad moment. He began to express his sympathy to everyone gathered to praise Boyce's life.

The memorial service began. The pastor spoke about God's grace and his love for humanity. He transitioned into the importance of forgiveness and how forgiveness is imperative to living a life pleasing to the Father. Although I was a member of the Methodist church across Second Avenue, I did enjoy listening to Michael speak because he was the city's pastor. Indeed, I would call him before my own pastor, as is true for most of the city.

Jackson stood and walked to the Steinway. He sat and opened the hymnal. His fingers pressed the keys with precision and beauty. The notes of *Amazing Grace* ascended into the ceiling of the sanctuary. As he played, Victoria began crying silently, and Auden placed his arm over her shoulders to comfort her.

I wondered why others were not present. I was not his biggest fan, but it was respectful to attend his service. I lived next door to him. I heard and saw some horrendous things happening in his backyard, but he was my neighbor. He was a human being, and I regretted not visiting him more often. I drove by his house numerous times and noticed him sitting on the porch; the only comfort was his walker with the two yellow tennis balls on the front feet. He sat there alone for the last moments of his life. It saddened me, but his anger chased away most of the neighbors.

Over the years, he and I had some amazing arguments. Boyce would not accept anyone telling him that he was wrong, especially a woman. He threatened to shoot me one time. I reached into my purse and produced a small pistol. He laughed and walked away. But, deep inside, Boyce was a good man. He found comfort in his army men, and they made him happy. I do wish he would have found that special person with whom to settle down, but maybe the strongest people are meant to go through life alone; perhaps those are the ones who can teach us the most about life. I missed the old bastard.

When Jackson finished the hymn, Michael invited everyone to stand for Boyce. Jackson began playing *How Great Thou Art*, Boyce's favorite hymnal. As he played, I heard tears in the silence.

Boyce

MY ASHES RESTED IN THE URN IN THE FRONT OF THE church. Victoria placed the oil portrait of me on the right, surrounded by other photographs that spanned my life. I was a handsome man in my earlier years. One of the photographs was taken by my mother when I was a child. She had died many, many years ago. But, that photograph always reminded me of growing up in Culpepper.

I grew up in Culpepper and went to Ole Miss where I majored in accounting. My college years were some of the best years of my life. I joined a fraternity, in which I was active until I was in my sixties. I was drawn to the idea of the brotherhood. When I graduated from college, I commissioned into the army as an officer. I rose to the rank of a Captain and decided that I had served my country long enough. When I was discharged from the army, I chose to return home and work for my family's mill.

I met Bronwyn shortly after I moved into my home on Magnolia. At first, we were simply friends, but our friendship grew into more. One evening after a night of martinis, he shared his true interest and feelings. I concurred with his, and we began our courtship. We were inseparable. We were incredibly discreet because of the social stigma of the times. We travelled a great deal because we could be ourselves away from the eyes of Culpepper. He was my best friend.

My eyes began searching the congregation. Aubrey walked into the church and sat with Jackson and the Harringtons. Although I made her cry often, I loved her. She was my salvation when I needed it the most. As she emptied the syringe, I could see the heartache in her eyes. She held my hand and wept as my soul left my body. She was a strong beautiful woman. Victoria was another guardian angel. I would have died years ago if she was not in my life. Like Aubrey, I caused Victoria so many tears. At times, I was malicious to her, but she and Auden were my support.

I glanced at Jackson. I am sure he never recognized me from his childhood. Bronwyn was fastidious about keeping us private. I rarely attended any of his family gatherings because we were both scared of people knowing about us.

My sight drifted among my friends. There were not many there, but the ones who attended did care about me in some manner. Most were not from the district, and I did not expect my neighbors to attend because most of the neighborhood had ejected me from their social circles. When I fell the first time, they began to turn their backs on me. There were times when I said hurtful things or behaved wrongfully to them, but my beloved had left me alone. I was angry at everyone. I was angry at God. Aubrey, Cara, and the Harringtons were the only neighborhood folks that cared for me. They were the only ones who loved me through my anger.

I did have a penchant for army men because there was a level

of comfort that I found in them. Most did not want a relationship because they would receive a dishonorable discharge for
engaging in such acts. I was an officer, so I understood the military lifestyle and the discretion in the brotherhood. The photographs began because of my fastidious personality. As the years
passed, the process became a game to see how many men would
allow a photo to be taken, and what the photo could contain.
I was shocked that a majority of the men allowed me to do it;
I am sure the alcohol added to their consenting. Bronwyn also
enjoyed men in uniform, and he volunteered to be the photog-
rapher when we were finished.

As Michael spoke, I heard Victoria's crying. I watched as she
collected her sadness with Auden's handkerchief. She was my
rock. I regretted all of the times that I made her cry because she
spent fifty cents more on a brand name. I hope she found the
letter that I left for her.

Jackson stood and walked toward the piano. He played well.
It reminded me of his uncle's playing, only better. A few weeks
ago, I sat in the parlor listening to Jackson play the piano that I
have not touched in years, while he sipped his bourbon that he
brought from his house because he knew that I was too cheap
for good bourbon.

As I watched him, he rarely glanced at the hymnal. He
played from memory, each note radiating through his mind. He
played from his soul for me.

When the piano silenced, a lone bugler from Fort Cullen
marched through the mahogany doors. He continued in perfect
step to the front of the sanctuary. He halted. He turned to the
congregation. As he stood beside my urn, he began playing Taps.
The notes ricocheted through the sanctuary.

Auden

BOYCE WANTED TO BE CREMATED, AND WE KNEW THE perfect place to leave him because Jackson had shared Bronwyn's memories. It was in the early twilight of the evening as I walked to Second Avenue and around First Baptist. I opened the old black wrought iron metal gate, and I entered the cemetery.

As I held the urn, tears appeared in my eyes. Boyce could be a hard personality for some people, but for me he was a dear close friend. For years, he and Victoria had been friends, and he welcomed me into his circle after Victoria and I married.

I collected myself. I heard voices and laughter, so I walked toward the noise, exchanged salutations with everyone, kissed my bride on her cheek, and placed Boyce on Bronwyn's marble headstone.

The martini Victoria made for me summoned me to it. It was significantly better than the ones Boyce prepared. Boyce refused to use the best liquor. Although he had the money, he would buy cheap vodka and place it in empty more expensive brand bottles, ones from my garbage.

We all began sharing stories of Boyce, and how he impacted

our lives. Aubrey spoke of him fondly, yet she appeared to be preoccupied with other mental demands. Jackson spoke of linguistically sparing with Boyce, which was always an entertaining event. It was admirable the way Jackson cared for Boyce. I do not know of any other neighbor who was willing to cut his hair and care for Boyce in that manner.

As we remembered Boyce, Victoria began crying. She loved him, and for the past two years, she has been his sole caretaker. She drove him to physician appointments, wrote checks for his accounts, and shared our meals with him. She was his guardian angel. I held her as the tears collected on my shirt.

After a few moments, we all took turns holding the urn and releasing him onto Bronwyn's final resting place, where in eternity they could finally be together. When Victoria had emptied the urn, we lifted our martini glasses and saluted the happiness of two of our friends.

Abby

CULPEPPER WAS AN INTERESTING TOWN. AS I WALKED down Magnolia, the surroundings captured my senses. The deep green magnolia leaves contrasted against the cloudless blue sky. Each lawn was perfectly showcased, and most of the homes were marked with a historic plaque. It was a beautiful neighborhood. I was walking to the end of Magnolia, where Dr. Harding owned a rental property. Jackson gave me a few phone numbers of possible property owners, and Dr. Harding had the only apartment available.

Jackson also gave me his number. I did not expect to meet such a man at the bar that night. We spent a few hours enjoying each other's company. We have been texting over the last few days, and we were planning to have dinner together this evening.

I reached the steps of the 401 Magnolia Avenue. It was a beautiful white colonial that Dr. Harding divided into four apartments, which was a shame. A tall out of shape man stepped from the front door. He raised his right hand and brushed his light brown hair to the right side of his head.

"Abby?"

"Yes, sir. Good evening."

He took my hand and kissed it, which I found odd. "Nice to meet you. I am Matthew Harding. Come in and check out the apartment."

I walked into the main entrance, and the first door on the right was open. The letter "A" rested two feet below the top of the door. I walked through the entrance, my heels thumped on the pine floors that were recently resurfaced. The living room was quite sufficient. To my right were two sets of double windows that stretched from the ceiling to the floor. In front of me were two more sets of double windows equal in size. There was a hallway on the far left of me and another door eight feet from the hallway on the same wall. I walked to the door and discovered a beautifully remodeled kitchen. Several windows lined the outside wall opposite a long counter, where the sink, the stove, and small appliances rested.

Matthew was standing behind me. As I turned around, his hand met the small of my back to guide me through the doorway into the living room. It rested there for a few moments too long. I walked down the hallway to two bedrooms and an updated bathroom. It was a great apartment for the year that I needed it.

As I left the apartment, I called Jackson to confirm that I was heading to the restaurant. He met me in front of his home, which was stunningly beautiful. The large columns across the front of the home reminded me of the homes in Charleston. I loved the beauty of those historic homes. Jackson walked out of his house as I was walking up to ring the bell. He was dressed in a pair of light brown Banana Republic chinos and a light pink polo. As he walked to me, he smiled. His hair was perfect, and his glasses suggested a level of intellectual elitism, although I had not experienced that with him.

We walked slowly north on Magnolia. He asked about my day, and if I was going to move into 401 Magnolia. He seemed to be a very caring individual, who was genuinely interested in others. As we walked into the commercial part of Magnolia, there was a man who was homeless sitting on a black iron bench. Jackson stopped and asked, "Daniel, how are you today?" He responded with a smile over his face.

We walked into an Italian steakhouse; there was an older white man with gray hair playing a baby grand piano in the corner. We were seated across from the dark mahogany bar. As the server walked over, a loud clap of thunder sounded, indicating a summer thunderstorm.

I sat listening to the piano while I enjoyed a glass of red wine. Jackson spoke of his day of writing and rummaging through his uncle's attic. He talked about growing up on this street and his mother. I inquired about his PhD dissertation and why he wanted to become a literary scholar. He loved literature and the way that literature made one feel. To him, there was power in language, and the aesthetic experience in language was one of the most beautiful experiences of all humanity. He taught because he wanted students to love Faulkner, O'Connor, and Williams. He wanted students to see the social truths embedded in southern literature. He mentioned reading Faulkner's Nobel Prize acceptance speech and the power of those words. For him, literature revealed a path to a better human existence. I admired his passion to his beliefs.

He asked about my childhood in Charleston and my family. I told him of growing up in the grocery store aisles. As a child, one of my best friends was the meat butcher in the first store my parents owned. I majored in Finance at William and Mary planning to work in the family business, but the banking industry captured me. I enjoyed my job, though it was hectic and mostly stressful.

After dinner we walked into the warm humidity. The smell of the recent storm permeated the air. We walked south on Magnolia. When we passed the awning for the coffee shop, Jackson noticed Daniel sitting on the sidewalk. He had retreated there for protection from the storm. Jackson walked over and handed him food. He shook his hand, and we continued our walk down Magnolia.

As we walked, Jackson pointed out where Dr. Harding and his wife, Shelby, lived. The front door was open, and we heard shouting from the opening. Matthew was screaming at Shelby about how disarranged the house was. He questioned what she did all day while he was providing a decent living for the family. He continued by attacking her appearances and recent weight gain. He was so overbearing that she was not able to respond to his hatred. We walked by as quickly as possible and crossed to the opposite side of the street.

Elizabeth and Patrick were sitting on their front porch having a bottle of wine. They waved and beckoned us to them. We opened the white wooden gate and walked to the front porch. Patrick Hathaway stood and Jackson introduced me to them. They invited us to sit on the porch, and Patrick and Jackson walked inside to retrieve two bourbons. The porch was large and inviting, with four white rocking chairs spaced perfectly across the porch. On the far left of the porch, a swing floated from left to right. There were four large square columns across the front of the home that supported the second floor balcony, which was the same shape and size as where we sat. Jackson returned. We sat in the swing facing the Hathaways.

Dr. Patrick Hathaway and his wife were part of the southern elite. Both were engrained in southern aristocracy. Patrick was a member of Junto, a men only club of intellectuals, who met once a month to discuss moral and philosophical challenges of society. Elizabeth was also a member of a female only book club comprised of the blue bloods of Culpepper. I could tell that Jackson adored the Hathaways. In many ways, he was very similar to them.

As we sat there, the darkness covered the streets. Lightning bugs began flickering in the median. An owl screeched in the sky above us. After two bourbons, Jackson and I shared our gratitude and excused ourselves. As we walked, the air became cooler. We made our way to his backyard.

We sat on the backyard swing. New bourbons rested in our palms. The lightning bugs flickered in the darkness. The moon rose slowly to the center of the darkened sky. I rested my head in his lap, gazing into the lawn. The quietness was reassuring as the dampness was beginning to permeate our surroundings. His right hand rested on my stomach. His presence gave me peace.

As I lay in his lap, the tree frogs begin to sing. The air was getting colder. I slowly became lost in the moment.

Victoria

I WALKED THE STEPS LEADING TO BOYCE'S PORCH. HIS death was now a week old. This was the first time that I have been able to enter his home. I was the executor of his will and financial affairs; thus, I needed to create an inventory of his belongings. I opened the door and walked into the kitchen. I knew what he owned in the public areas of his home, but I needed to enter the basement and view its contents; it was a place that was off limits to guests, and I always abided by his wishes. I opened the door leading downstairs.

Cautiously, I stepped downward until I reached the basement floor. The room was incredibly organized. It was an open room, but there was a living space with a brown leather sofa and matching chairs. The space also contained a fifty-two inch flat screen television. Adjacent to the living space, there was a wet bar that contained numerous bottles of alcohol. Across the room, there was an open door that led to a bathroom, with a large walk-in shower with multiple shower heads.

I walked toward the wall of cabinets on the northern side of the room. I opened two doors where I found a cabinet full of brown cardboard boxes that were the size of a shoebox. Each of the boxes was labeled with a specific year. The years began in 1975, which was the year that Boyce bought the house and moved into the historic district. He was in his early forties. I reached up and clutched one box labeled 1975a. Curiously, I opened the box, and the contents shocked me. I closed the box, and captured year 1980c. It contained the same type of items. I pulled a few more years out of the cabinet. All of the boxes contained the same items. There were thousands of them. My hands were shaking. I have known Boyce for thirty years.

I continued searching the basement for items that were listed in his will, but my mind was still trapped by the contents of those boxes. There were thousands of Polaroid photographs of naked young army men taken in different places in his house. In some of the photographs, Boyce was engaged in carnal activities. After the 2007 boxes, he printed off pictures from his cell phone, but the depictions remained the same. Some years had five or more boxes that contained the documentation of his conquests. In total, there must have been thousands.

My heart ached, and my stomach became uneasy. I wondered how many of these young men were inebriated during the encounters, or were they all uninhibited consenters. In the midst of my nausea, I heard the doorbell.

I returned upstairs, and closed the basement door as I exited. Aubrey was standing at the door. I opened the door and invited her into the house. She noticed my car parked on the street and decided to stop.

"Oh Victoria, I know it must be so difficult for you right now. Is there anything that I can help you with?"

"Thank you, Aubrey. I greatly appreciate your kindness, but

Sally is coming over this afternoon to help me organize his things. I have called everyone that he has left something to. It's a process."

As she hugged me, "Okay honey, if you need anything at all, please call me. I don't mind helping at all."

She turned and walked outside; I followed her. I stood on the porch as she drove away. I loved Aubrey, and there was so much that needed to be done, but I needed to preserve Boyce's reputation. Appearances were most important to him; I could not let everyone know of the photographs that are buried downstairs; I am sure they were only the beginning of his secrets.

Ms. Sally

BOYCE HAD SOME NASTY PICTURES. I DON'T KNOW what to do with him. There were so many pictures of young naked Army men. I just can't believe he did that. We were cleaning his house and found another box in the basement. I wasn't scared to open it cause of all the other boxes. It couldn't be worse than the others. We found letters from Old Man Bronwyn. This damn man was fooling everybody, but he didn't have a choice. People would have killed him if they knew the truth.

When I was cleaning, I noticed that I had not dusted the fireplace. So, I walked over and started picking up the pictures and what nots. There were two small statues on each end of the mantel. They were mounted, so I just wiped the one on the left. When I touched the one on the right, it clicked. I called Auden over, and he found a door that opened into a tunnel.

Auden couldn't leave well enough alone. We walked into that tunnel for a few feet. There was another door, but it was locked.

Auden

I PULLED THE BOXES OFF THE SHELF FOR MS. SALLY
to empty in the garbage bags. When we found the other boxes
in the far right cabinet, I knew they were not pictures because
they were not labeled with a year. I picked up the brown boxes
that were similar sizes of the picture boxes. I opened the lid,
and dust floated upward. I found cards and letters addressed to
Boyce. I opened one envelope slowly and unfolded it.

Dearest Boyce,

*It has been a wonderful 25 years. I have enjoyed all of our
travels and our times together. My life is forever changed and
better for knowing you. You are a beautiful soul.*

With Love,
Bronwyn

Boyce saved all of his letters and cards. It was touching to
read some of them. Their love was hidden for nearly 40 years.

Yet, they endured. I wonder if Bronwyn knew of Boyce's photography collection.

We continued cleaning the cabinets. All of his pictures were discarded, and Bronwyn's letters were placed in a box for storage at my house. Ms. Sally continued while I ascended the stairs to examine the rest of the house. I walked around reading all of the Broadway artifacts in his home. As I walked into the library, I imagined my friend reading in his chair. He loved language as much as he loved history. I sat in his chair while the tears filled my eyes. I missed him. I wondered how many martinis he had sitting in this chair reading. He sat alone in this house so many nights in the last two years of his life. The neighborhood simply discarded him. He only had us and Aubrey, and maybe Cara on occasion, visit with him.

I glanced around the room; my eyes fixated on the white grand piano in the other room. At that moment, I realized why he stopped playing the piano and why he became so angry. It was the same year that Bronwyn died. Bronwyn and he would take turns playing in front of their friends to prove who was better. Bronwyn was better, but I would never tell Boyce the truth. When Bronwyn died, a 40 year old relationship ended. His best friend was gone. For weeks, Boyce lay in bed. He refused to leave his house. He feigned being sick. In reality, he was in mourning.

Damn, I missed him. As I sat there, my mind remembered images that were taken in this room. Ms. Sally's scream called me to the basement.

Ms. Sally discovered the fireplace was a door that opened into an underground tunnel. I hoped my face did not reveal the truth.

Joshua

I SAW THE PEOPLE WALKING IN THE STREET WHILE we were buying food from Mr. James. I asked mommy who they were. She said they were people who hated other people. I asked if they hated me. They don't hate me. I asked who. Mommy said they hated Ms. Sally. I love Ms. Sally. She is nice to me. She takes care of me sometimes. Why would they hate her? Mommy gave me a peach to eat. I love peaches. The man in white was walking closer to me. He was waving a flag. It was loud. People were screaming. The man holding the flag was screaming. He came closer. Mommy took my hand, and she pulled me away from the man. Everybody was screaming. People over there were screaming. Man in the street was screaming. Mommy, there is Ms. Sally. Why is she screaming? They were screaming at each other. I was scared. Everyone was screaming. Mommy picked me up and we ran. We ran fast. I dropped my peach, but it's okay. Mommy dropped our food. We ran into the store. A rock broke the glass. We ran to the back. More rocks. Glass fell. People were screaming. We ran to the very back. Mommy squeezed me hard. It was hard to breathe. People were in the store. They threw stuff outside the store. We ran to the back and outside. We ran in the little street. It stunk. We ran by a garbage can. I pinched my nose. We ran to a bigger street. The screaming was whispering. I didn't see the man with the flag or Ms. Sally. We were almost to our home. Mommy turned around. She put me down. I cried. I sat on the sidewalk and cried. I don't know why I was crying. I just cried. Mommy held me. She held me hard. It was hard to breathe. I think she wanted to cry too.

Auden

I REACHED DOWN AND GRASPED THE SUNDAY PAPER. The headline on the front page read, "Rioters Destroy Downtown, Stores Looted, and Several Hospitalized." I stood there for a few moments and read the front page.

Saturday morning the Klan held a rally and marched downtown in the commercial section of Magnolia. As the march rolled south on Magnolia, the sea of white robes divided the supporters from the protestors. As the white sea moved south, the groups on either side flowed with them. When they reached the midway point of the commercial district, the area where the farmers market is held every Saturday, the actions of both crowds escalated.

I was standing at the end of the market purchasing tomatoes, when I heard the rock shatter the pharmacy's store front window. The mobs erupted violently against each other. I turned south and ran home as quickly as possible. Victoria was in the front yard attending to a flower garden. We rushed into the house, leaving her tools beside the plants.

Our home was the second home on the right as one enters

136

into the historic district. The riot was only two blocks away, and I was afraid the mob would enter the district and destroy our property. We stood in the parlor staring into the lawn and waited for the chaos. As we stood, the police sirens ricocheted through the air. It gave us hope. The crowds crossed over the street and moved toward the district, as if running from the police. As they came closer, it was apparent the crowd consisted of mostly young white men. Two of the white men reached for our neighbor's mailbox and wrestled it from its foundation. Another white man appeared with a baseball bat. They destroyed our mailbox and crossed onto our lawn. I stood in the parlor glancing out the window holding the pistol in my right hand. Victoria spoke frantically to the 911 operator.

Others in the mob continued running through the historic district. Some ran to First or Second Avenue; some continued on Magnolia. Police officers on horseback were the force behind their running.

When the crowd disseminated, a police officer walked across our lawn to the front porch. I placed the gun on the table in the foyer, and I opened the door. We immediately remembered each other. He was checking on any damage in the district. I invited him in and introduced him to Victoria.

I poured the officer a bourbon, and we sat in the library. His father and I were at Ole Miss Law together. His father was one of my closest friends over the years. He passed away a few years ago from pancreatic cancer. He and his family lived in Jackson, so his son joined the force in Culpepper to remain close to home. While we were reminiscing his father, Victoria walked into the library with a platter covered with food.

I loved that about Victoria. She was the most hospitable

person I have ever met. She genuinely wanted people to feel welcome in our home. She was an excellent chef. She was an accomplished attorney and a well-respected judge, but her food was beyond amazing. Victoria grew up in Culpepper. Her father was a physician and her mother was nurse, but her grandfather and great grandfather were mill owners in Culpepper. She was ingrained in southern society, and I am not sure why she chose me to love her, but I was indebted to her. She was my rock.

We sat in the library with our bourbon and her food until the radio called him away to more important causes.

Jackson

I ENJOYED SPENDING TIME WITH ABBY. SHE WAS A very special woman. Abigail Brooke Rhodes was born in Charleston, South Carolina a few years after I was born in Culpepper. Her parents owned a chain of grocery stores across South Carolina and Georgia. She attended William and Mary, where she majored in Finance. She has worked for the same bank for her entire career, though in different positions. Currently, she is a vice president of branch services. She is expecting to live in Culpepper for a year.

She had a way of making me feel comfortable, almost peaceful. As we lay on the sofa on the screened in porch of the lake house, I could feel her breathing as I held her, her back to my chest. The night crickets began the nightly symphony. The tree frogs joined the orchestra. The song of a nearby owl added to the melody. The music harmonized with our souls. Abby was drifting off to sleep. .

After having lunch together this afternoon, I invited her to the lake house to enjoy the water. For dinner, I grilled two Porterhouse steaks. Although it has been a short period of time, I was growing fonder of her daily. She possessed a rare ability of maintaining my focus, which has always been a challenge in past relationships. She was an intellectual, which elicited a desire to spend time with her. She wanted to help the poor and make a difference in her community, which I loved.

I rested in the calmness of the night contemplating the discovered secrets of my family. The Klan parade today caused memories of Big Daddy to surface. I still do not understand how such a loving man was responsible for so many brutally beaten individuals. As they marched today, a crowd of people screamed and supported their ideology. They waved their flags and signs inscribed with racism. The street where Big Daddy taught me to ride my bicycle, where I fell numerous times and scratched my body, that street was the place of hatred and intolerance.

Abby and I were at the market when the people began to converge downtown. We watched the crowds of people standing on the sidewalk. Their shouts astonished me. I wondered how many of my neighbors longed to stand in the crowd. How many would be there if appearances did not matter? I felt uneasy about the whole situation. Perhaps, it was the memories of Big Daddy. Abby and I left before the march began.

As we lay in the calmness of the darkness, Faulkner walked through the doorway. He began sniffing the night air as a slight breeze blew over from the lake. His head vacillated up and down as the new smells entered his body. After a few minutes, he positioned himself on the floor. He lay on his side, and within a few moments, we were both dreaming.

I woke Sunday morning to the smell of fresh coffee and Abby's fingers running through my hair. Faulkner was already running through the backyard chasing squirrels and other dreams he would probably never catch.

We drove back to the district after breakfast. I drove her home, and I returned home to dress for church. Church has always been a large part of my life. There was solace in knowing that there was something larger with a purpose that guided my life. As an adult, I still believed in that purpose, though at times my level of faith seemed to lessen.

I walked in late as the choir was singing the Hallelujah Chorus. The beautiful voices radiated God's love and grace. I stood in the back of the sanctuary, unable to move. I was mesmerized by the emotions of the moment. When they sat, I walked up the stairs to the balcony. There was a sense of calmness that the balcony gave to me. I sat down staring at the 200 year old pipe organ extending from the floor to the ceiling. The sun permeating the stain glass windows stole my view for a few moments.

The pianist began playing, and a violinist joined her. Together, the notes moved us all. My soul stood still to listen. As they played *Amazing Grace*, I remembered the joys of growing up in this church. I remember my mother sitting on the seventh pew every Sunday, with all of us sitting with her. I remember her crying when Sarah Beth married at that altar. The joys of remembering took me from the pastor's sermon. My mind was lost in the tranquility of my childhood.

Michael

GOOD MORNING. WELCOME TO FIRST BAPTIST. WE ARE so glad you are here this morning. If you are visiting with us, please make yourself at home. We are glad that you are here. If you need anything, please locate an usher. Over the next month, we will examine the role of grace in people's lives and in our community. Grace is an important attribute of a Christian's life. Grace is paramount to a relationship with God. Without grace, there is nothing.

And, grace is not simply a New Testament ideal. Joseph's story is inundated with grace. His brothers hated him. He was sold into slavery and thought he would die in prison. But, God had other plans, and grace is described in Genesis 45:7, "But God sent me ahead of you to preserve for you a remnant on earth and to save your lives by a great deliverance." What a beautiful story of grace.

Next, grace is found in the lives of the Israelites. They complained and disobeyed God countless of times. Often, they chose to follow their own desires rather than His plan. Yet, God provided protection, manna, and eventually they entered into the Promised Land. That's grace folks.

There was a young man named David who slew a giant with a stone and a sling. He became king. He was a murderer and an adulterer. But, he loved God, and God loved him. He was the apple of God's eye. He made some bad decisions. But, God forgave him. That's grace.

Rehab was a prostitute who hid two spies who were sent to spy on Jericho. Rehab hid the two spies and lied to her leaders, when questioned about them. She confessed her belief in God and sought His mercy. Her family was spared, and she served God the rest of her life.

The New Testament is also full of depictions of grace. The story of the prodigal son and his return home is a beautiful story of grace. The father ran to him and hugged him. He did not simply wait for his son to come to him. He ran to him and embraced him and said, "My son has come home." There is more to it, though. In that time, the father knew that it was inappropriate for the father to run to his son. It was frowned upon. But, he denied society and ran to his son. There was a great celebration, and it was all restored.

Once Jesus was walking through Samaria, and he stopped at Jacob's well. He sat because he was tired. When the Samarian woman walked up, Jesus asked for a drink of water. She was shocked. She questioned his logic. He was Jewish, and he asked a Samarian woman for a drink. The story continues. He knew her. He knew her past. Grace abounded.

Saul was headed to Damascus to persecute followers of Christ. On his way, a light came from the sky. Saul was blinded, and he later becomes one of the greatest followers of Christ. Grace. Simply grace.

Grace is not simply a term that resides only in theological

texts. Rather, grace is an action that must accompany our daily lives. We have become a world that is incredibly disconnected from our fellow man. When I grew up, we cared for our neighbors. We cared for people we did not know. If a person was hurting, we comforted that person. Today, people are different. Today, grace is confined to our best friends or our closest family members. When was the last time that you showed your neighbor grace? When was the last time that you stopped and asked the man who is homeless if he needed anything? We have become so separated from each other in our communities that we have forgotten that we must love people where they are. We must love people in their situation, because love and grace are connected.

We live in chaotic times. People are hurting. People need grace. For that reason, we are dedicating the next month to truly examining the role grace should play in our daily lives.

Please stand if you are able. The doors of the church are open if you feel God is leading you to become part of this church family. As the choir sings, let's pause and examine how our own lives reflect grace.

Corbin

I LEFT ERIC AND EMILY'S HOUSE AROUND 10:00 SUN-
day evening. I was the last person to leave. They invited a few
neighbors over for drinks. Phoebe came, and it was not as awkward as I thought it would be. Aubrey was there as well, but
no one knows about us. Matthew and Shelby were there for a
few hours. Cara came late, as was common with her. She was
always late and unprepared. Last year, the neighborhood had a
progressive Christmas party. Auden and Victoria were the first
house where everyone gathered for drinks and the first course
of food. After their home, the group moved to Cara's house.
Cara had not prepared anything. We sat in her living room
for nearly an hour while she worked frantically in the kitchen.
Aubrey and a few others joined her to assist. I and a few others
returned to my aunt's home and remained for the rest of the
evening. Everyone could always trust that my aunt would have
an impeccable gathering.

It was interesting that I have engaged in some type of sexual
relationship with every female that was present tonight. I smiled

when the thought appeared in my mind. I was amazed that no one ever revealed our secrets. Shelby and Emily were both married, but the others were single.

Emily and Eric did have their sexual secrets. Every few months the couple would travel to Jackson for the weekend for their monthly club meeting. They had joined a swingers club a few years ago. It needed to be far enough away to maintain appearances for her social climbing. I did hate that Emily cared so strongly about social acceptance. Tonight, she mentioned she was having dinner next week with the mayor, who is a Culpepper blue blood. His family owned one of the mills in town for several generations. Emily found importance in mentioning her social meetings whenever possible.

She and my aunt had a horrible argument a few weeks ago. Emily and my aunt have been slowly drifting apart for months. My aunt became tired of Emily's antics and her own ideas of self-importance. My aunt is incredibly engrained Culpepper, and at first, she genuinely cared for Emily and wanted to mentor her into an appropriate member of society. For years, Emily sought her counsel in all social matters. In so many ways, Emily wanted to become Victoria, but Emily's new found money and status would always be an obstacle to the Culpepper's social society.

My aunt grew up in this town. She is somehow connected to Mary Harriman who founded the Junior League, and her great grandmother helped establish the first Junior League in Culpepper. She attended Vanderbilt's law school. She is the brightest woman that I know. Auden is my mother's brother. Auden grew up 30 minutes south of Culpepper in a small country town. His family has owned one of the largest grocery store chains east of the Mississippi for several generations. They are truly meant for each other.

I left Eric and Emily's and walked to Aubrey's, the late summer air was a bit cooler.

Abby

THE AUTUMN AIR WAS REFRESHING. BEING FROM Charleston, the hot humid summers in Mississippi can be overbearing. The new cooler air was a welcome to the district because it brought southern football with it, which meant a number of neighborhood rivalries. I was walking to Jackson's house to walk with him to the Harrington's home. Auden and Victoria were having a football party to cheer on Ole Miss, who was playing Arkansas. For food, Auden made his famous pork ribs and pork tenderloin in honor of the Arkansas Razorbacks. It was the perfect late October football game.

When I walked up to him, he kissed me lightly. As we walked north on Magnolia to the Harrington's home, he cradled my hand in his, our fingers intertwined. In so many ways, he complimented me. Though it had been only a few months, I was growing fond of him.

As we walked into the home, Victoria greeted us in the foyer wearing a black and gold cotton vest, with a gold "V" in the top left corner that covered a white Burberry button down. Her pearls were positioned perfectly around her neck and matched the strand around her wrist. Even on football Saturdays, she was elegant.

We walked into the home, Auden was walking through the backdoor holding a platter of ribs. His brown chinos and a navy blue button down with Ole Miss embroidered in cardinal red on the shirt pocket. He was screaming "Hotty Toddy," which he often did during football games. Auden was an incredible supporter of the university, financially and in other manners. When Ole Miss lost, which they did quite often for the past few years, Auden would enter a state of mourning. He was hoping this year would be better because the university had hired one of Alabama's coaches as the Ole Miss head coach.

Sarah Beth was sitting in the parlor with Gavin. She was proudly wearing her Agnes Scott shirt. Gavin was dressed in Boston College attire. Jackson and I walked over and exchanged small talk with them for a few minutes. Afterward, we walked from the parlor into the living room, where a large 55-inch television was mounted on the wall opposite the room's entrance. Matthew and Shelby sat on the sofa, both wearing Mississippi State polos. Patrick and Elizabeth were sitting in the chairs that flanked the beautiful marble gas fireplace. Elizabeth was exquisite. Her legs were crossed. She wore a navy blue Versace skirt with a Lilly Pulitzer button down that she had embroidered with "Ole Miss." Several strings of pears draped from her neck down to her chest. To her right, Patrick sat in another Queen Anne chair, his legs crossed as well. He wore perfectly pressed brown khakis with a navy blue starched button down shirt. His Ole Miss bow tie was the perfect accent. They sat holding Waterford glasses filled with bourbon.

Aubrey was standing in the kitchen discussing local gossip

with Cara. Both were casually dressed in brown khakis and Ole Miss pullovers. Grace and Sawyer Huntingdon stood at the granite counter sipping bourbon and arguing with Auden about southern football. They were one of the seven Arkansas graduates in the home. It was humorous to watch an Arkansas graduate devour the pork ribs. Grace graduated from the university with a degree in Art History, though she did not plan to use her training for employment purposes. Sawyer attended Arkansas for his undergraduate and his medical degree. They were both retired and spent most of the year traveling.

There were twenty other people in the house, all of whom I had met, but we were simply acquaintances. Eric and Emily were absent because they were visiting friends in Jackson, which surprised me because Emily seldom missed such an opportunity. Jackson and I rotated through the house reintroducing ourselves to many of those acquaintances. At one point in the living room, I noticed Shelby was not sitting beside Matthew, which rarely happened at these gatherings, but Matthew was entering the inebriation stage of his evening.

At 7:30, the game began, with a majority of the living room members screaming "Hotty Toddy." I retrieved Jackson and me a fresh Woodford, and as I stood in the kitchen, I noticed Shelby walking out of the cottage in the back lawn, which was where Corbin lived. She walked briskly to the side of the house, past the side lawn opposite the living room, and entered through the front door. When she appeared in front of Matthew with a fresh beer, Matthew accepted it with gratitude. He did not realize how long she had been away. A few moments later, Corbin appeared in the sun room at the back of the house.

At half time, the Arkansas fans were ecstatic. Ole Miss was

losing terribly. Jackson and I excused ourselves and retreated to Uncle Bronwyn's.

As we walked into the house, Jackson walked into the parlor and prepared us a drink. The Waterford glasses were heavy. They were beautiful. The bottom was concentrated with small diamond patterns that reached to the middle of the sides on the glass. From the middle, several slender oval patterns vertically connected the diamonds to the top of the glass. For Jackson, bourbon was better in nice crystal.

Bronwyn bequeathed the house and all of its contents to Jackson. All of the Waterford was easily worth thousands of dollars. In addition to the seventy pieces in the parlor, there was an entire wall of crystal in the kitchen.

I was beginning to care for Jackson. I loved how he treated me as if I was the most important person in the room, even when we both knew I was not. He always treated me with kindness. I enjoyed his chivalrous nature. Although we were moving incredibly fast, it felt right. I was slowly allowing him closer to me, which I had not done in quite a long while.

We walked into the den. He took my glass and placed it on the coaster on the table, and repeated the action with his own glass. He hugged and kissed me. We laid on the sofa and started watching the movie.

Elizabeth Hathaway

I HAVE HAD A FEW BOURBONS. OLE MISS IS LOSING TO a horrible football team. What the hell is wrong with this new coach? He's from Alabama. He was supposed to be the light leading us out of the darkest time in our football history. He's an idiot. Oh Sarah Beth. She is such a stunningly beautiful woman, and Gavin is such a dapper young gentleman. I didn't realize that she went to Agnes Scott. When my sister went there it was an excellent school. Now, it's just a plethora of lesbians. Her father was something else. He was the leader of the neighborhood mafia when he was alive, which was a group of self-righteous, egotistical, power hungry historic district citizens. There were approximately seven of them. Individually, they joined all of the major board of directors for organizations that impacted life in the district. Her father was a ruthless son of a bitch. How he became a state Supreme Court judge I will never understand. I think Eric is now the head of the group, and he doesn't have enough sense to come in out of the rain. Everyone knows Emily has cheated on him. I have friends who have seen Emily engaged in questionable behavior, so I know they are not simply rumors.

Aubrey looks incredibly relaxed this evening. I wonder why that is. Normally, she is dressed up to the nine. Oh Corbin. That is one simpleminded young man. I do not understand for the life of me how he graduated from Ole Miss. Apparently, they have lowered their standards since I was there. I will never understand why Victoria allowed him to move into her cottage behind the house. I live next door, and I see what goes on over there. Corbin has turned that little cottage into a den of fornication.

Victoria is such a kind soul. She cared for that old unpleasant Boyce the last few years of his life. He didn't have anyone else because he chased them all away with his odious behavior. She never left him, even when he was horrible to her. She cared for that man until he took his last breath.

Jackson and Abby went home. He was such a handsome young man, and Abby was not worthy of him. She appears too blue collar. Jackson needs another academic or physician, someone who can handle his intellectualism. I loved his mother. We were such good friends. We met in the Junior League many, many years ago. Her stationery was divine. I assured her that I would look after Sarah Beth and the others.

Why did Patrick give me another bourbon? Patrick is the love of my life. We have had an interesting journey, but we have always been there for each other. He loved me through four miscarriages. He was a good man. Matthew and Shelby are not as lucky. They try to hide it, but we all know their marriage is drowning like a drunk rat in the sewer, which is what happens when one begins a marriage after an affair. But, there is more to their relationship, and I simply cannot place my finger on it.

Oh Lord be still. Julie and Seth just walked in, hours too late. The game is in the third quarter. They just moved into the

JOSEPH R. JONES

district a year ago. Apparently, he comes from some money, but he will not receive it until his mother dies. They purchased a house on the south side of the district hoping that the mother dies soon. She is a complete gold digger. Bless her white trash heart. They moved from Tupelo to Culpepper, which makes no sense to me either. Honestly, I am not sure why Victoria invited them.

Ole Miss is losing terribly, and it is time that Patrick and I left. Auden has slipped into a football mourning period.

Patrick Hathaway

THE DRIVEWAY WAS TOO STEEP. THE DARKNESS OF the night was spinning. I couldn't walk down the incline. Ole Miss lost. Damn. Fire the coach. Where's the machine when you really need them. They would get rid of him. The driveway was too steep. One step at a time Auden kept telling me. I held on to him as I walked slowly. One foot in front of the other. Slowly. The driveway was too damn steep. Where is Elizabeth? Oh, she is with Corbin in front of us. She is so beautiful. There are days when I still can't believe that woman married me, even more days when I can't believe she stayed all of these years. She still has my heart. I hope she holds on to it.

She feels so badly, but the doctors all told her it was not her fault. There are other ways she yelled through the sobbing tears. All these years later, I know she still blames herself. These two young men taking care of us old folks, walking us home. I didn't mean to drink so much, but those bourbons went down so smoothly. Damn Ole Miss. Damn them.

Whit was outside rambling again. We walked through the door of our home, and Auden and Corbin walked away. As I

155

closed the door, my bride stood in the foyer staring at me. Methodically, I walked to her. I placed my old wrinkled hands on her porcelain cheeks. She was so beautiful. She walked closer and kissed my forehead. I will never deserve her love.

Whit

HEY YOU. YOU FOUR WALKING RIGHT THERE. WHY don't you listen to me? Hey, the four of you, listen to me. The rain is coming. The rain is going to wash the dirt off the red hard bricks. You will be able to see the bright red color of the bricks because the rain will take the dirt with it. Come sit with me. The grass is safe. The rain is coming. Sit with me in the grass. Come sit with me in the grass before the rain comes.

Jackson

THE NEXT MORNING AFTER THE FOOTBALL PARTY, I walked Abby home after we attended church. When I walked into Uncle Bronwyn's, I decided it was time to venture into the attic again. As I opened the attic door, the wind from the moving door propelled dust and dirt into the air. It floated in the morning sunlight. As I stood watching the haze of dust, I noticed a tint of gray rising in the air. I walked over to the window and glanced into the morning air. My face froze, staring into the historic district. I ran down the two flights of stairs and out of the front door. Whit was running across the median. He reached the house moments before I did.

He grabbed a ladder, which he positioned on the second floor balcony. In a split second, he ascended the ladder and wrapped his right arm around the child, who was screaming through tears. Together, they seemed to slide down the side rails skipping several rungs. He placed her on the ground and retreated back to the balcony, where he grasped a small pure bred Pomeranian. With the same sudden escape, he landed on the ground with the puppy.

I carried the puppy and the child across the red brick street to the median while comforting both. When I moved my focus from them, Whit was no longer around. I glanced through the crowd of neighbors. I couldn't locate their hero.

Eric and Emily darted over to us. Emily's joy was released in bursts of screaming and tears as she held her youngest child. She was frantic realizing what had happened. Eric stood stoically in the median staring into the dark gray smoke of his burning dreams. The fire truck sirens never broke his concentration. His dreams crumbled among the black and gray smoke. Tears rolled down his face. I have never seen him so distraught. He was always jovial and nonchalant about life and what it offered him. His disposition was now antithetical. I could see the fear in him. It was a fear beyond the fire and the loss of property. He was so fixated on the property that he rarely acknowledged his child or his wife. He simply stood in the midst of his neighbors silently broken.

When they married, they decided to purchase the Hollingsworth house in the district. It was a beautiful house whose décor was imprisoned in the early sixties. After remodeling the house, they moved into the district and began making a family. Emily bore three children, the youngest was the girl whom Whit saved from the balcony.

The median filled with neighbors. We all stood staring through the loss, seeking the brightness of the sun, only to view the smoke darkening the blue skies of the historic district.

As the house continued burning, the smell of reality became apparent on Eric's face. He lowered his body and crouched in the median. His face filled with huge drops of perspiration. He fell backwards; the ground catching his body.

Eric

MY HEAD SWAM. I NEEDED TO LIE DOWN. MY BODY
went limp. The ground hurt. I could hear people screaming for
the EMTs to help me through the chaos of the fire. My house
was burning down.

I have not paid homeowner's insurance in three months. I
let the policy lapse because of other debts in the business. My
action was overlooked at The Bank of Culpepper because my
best friend was one of the vice presidents. I promised him that
I would reinstate the insurance as soon as the other financial
obligation was met, but reality now lay with me in the grass of
the median.

The EMT touched my face slightly. I wanted to remain
lifeless on the grass. I wanted it all to go away. Emily deserved
better. My kids deserved better. I wanted to be a better pro-
vider.

I grew up two counties over. I remember living in an old
white house with no plumbing. It was the early 70s, and poor-
er parts of the state still had outhouses. We had two because
we were such a big family. During the winter nights, we would

relieve ourselves in a five gallon bucket, and each morning one of
the older boys would take it out and empty it in one of the houses. We normally took cold baths, unless momma heated pans of
water on the stove for the ruthless winter nights. We shared bath
water from youngest to oldest, because the oldest was always the
one who was the dirtiest.

I shared a room with two of my older brothers, Jake and
Michael. I learned what I needed to know from them. I discovered sex from their hidden magazines that they stole from our
father. I woke up one night and Jake was looking at one and was
touching himself. I didn't really understand it, but I looked up
to him. The next day I found the magazine and did exactly what
he was doing. I understood. I started to steal my own magazines
from our father, who obviously realized what was happening. I
hid my magazines in the woods far beyond the outhouses. An
old generic Tupperware container became the magazines' storage locker. I didn't want to share with them.

We were poor, but we loved each other.

He grasped the back of my neck with his hand, supporting
my head. Slowly, I sat erect. Emily gave me a bottle of water. The
coolness did nothing for my sin. I sat in the cool autumn morning air. I sat there realizing the pain that I had caused my family,
wondering what was next.

The smoke continued to rise into the air. The smell of burning wood filled the entire district. I glanced around, and I saw
all of my neighbors. Victoria was hugging Emily. Auden walked
over and offered his hand to help me stand. Emily was crying,
and Victoria held her like they were old friends. Others began
to place hands on Emily's back and shoulders. Too, they tried to
comfort her.

The water rushed into the second floor balcony and windows. Three trucks surrounded my house. We all just stood in the median watching them trying to save my house. I just watched, knowing there was nothing I could do.

Jackson

THE CHAOS OF THE FIRE CHASED US FROM THE DIS-trict. After hours, the smell of burnt old wood was unpleasant. Abby and I decided to spend the Sunday evening at the lake house. We loved the placidity of the lake.

We sat on the dock with our feet dangling off the side, slightly grazing the surface of the warm water with our toes. The sun settling into the horizon. The bright red and orange colors streaked through the evening sky, reaching into the lake. As we sat there drying in the remaining sun, I reached and brought her into my shoulder. She leaned into my chest. My arm wrapped around her back and cupping on her shoulder. I glanced into the setting sun as I was falling in love with her. She complemented me in ways that others had not. I could feel her chest rise and fall with each breath. Holding her comforted me.

I glanced behind us and noticed Faulkner running at full speed toward us. He was two years old. When he was born, I chose him because of his green eyes, which many thought would change as he aged. At two, it was apparent his eyes would remain the same radiant color. For the first ten weeks of his life, I drove

20 miles every Saturday to play with him. During each visit, he became more comfortable with me, as I did with him. As he grew, we became best friends.

He ran onto the dock and wedged his nose between Abby and me. He was a persistent lad.

Abby and I stood and walked up the hill through the back door, onto the screened in porch. We loved to sleep on the sofa together there. The air was cool blowing from the lake. The symphony of nature was calming. But, this time she wanted to hear me play the piano.

I walked into the den of the lake house where a baby grand sat quietly. I walked over to a mahogany bookcase that contained thousands of songs. I glanced carefully over my choices. I chose Eric Clapton. As I sat on the black leather bench, Abby approached me with a bourbon. She sat beside me. I opened the book, and she chose the song. I smiled and kissed her softly. My fingers began pressing the keys with poise and precision. I was shocked at how well I played. As the music filled the small den, Abby began to sing. Her voice was angelic. As I listened to her, I was lost in the tranquility of it all. We sat for an hour, drinking, playing, and singing.

Faulkner broke our connection and reminded us that he was in the room. I stood and walked to the back porch to open the door for him to go outside. She retreated to the kitchen.

We all returned into the living room. Abby and I lay on the sofa. I was behind her and held her as the movie began. Faulkner lay on the floor. The crunching of the stick in his mouth was a reminder of his innocence.

As I lay there, I began thinking about Thanksgiving in two weeks. It would be the first time in years that our family gathered under one roof. I smiled. We would be together.

The next morning, I decided to run through the woods around the lake. There was an old dirt path that has existed all of my life. It was a cool fall morning. The leaves were changing. The bright yellow and red colors captured my eyes as I ran past them. The dirt sounded odd under my shoes. I ran without my music. The wind blew vicariously through the trees, causing the leaves to fall slowly to the chilling ground. The cracking noises of dried leaves and limbs reverberated from my soles. There were fewer birds calling out through the treetops. The sound of death permeated the air.

I ran slowly. The silence engendered memories that inundated my mind. When my grandmother reached the appropriate age, my mother began hosting Thanksgiving dinner. On that Thursday, strangers would begin arriving around noon. Many of these family members were cousins or others whom I only saw on an annual occasion.

The meal was always perfect. My mother was an excellent chef. I hated turkey, so she would also cook a huge ham covered in honey and pineapple rings just for me, though my annual cousins often ate most of it. I loved the smell of Thanksgiving. I never understood how thirty or forty different items cooked in the same space could combine to produce such a heavenly smell. I also never understood how there could be enough crystal and matching plates to feed everyone, but there always was.

My mother would spend days cooking dinner. Thanksgiving was a time for all of us to remember the joys of our blessings, and how lucky we were to be born into this family. She believed that we were lucky to be Kensingtons.

I paused for a moment and stood staring across the lake. The early morning sun glistened off the water. I removed my shoes and my shirt. I walked to the bank and slowly entered the water. The coldness covered the surfaces of my body. Methodically, I lowered myself into the cold dark water. I leaned forward and swam away from the bank. The coldness became comforting. I began to float in the water with my back lying carelessly on the surface. My mind rested in the calmness of the lake.

Blake

THE UBER DRIVER STOPPED QUICKLY IN FRONT OF THE home. I stepped out of the car with my bags. He drove away as I stood staring at the house. The American flag was on one side and the Ole Miss flag was on the opposite side. The rocking chairs were perfectly placed on the porch. The ceiling fans were operating, even for a late November day. I wanted to walk to the door, but the memories of this house flooded me. I paused. This place was my second home. It was my home when my father kicked me out because I was not good enough for him. It had been years since I was here. I never had the strength to tell my siblings the real reasons. They still do not know how Uncle Bronwyn became my hero. A single tear formed and rolled from my eye down my cheek. The door opened, and Jackson smiled and ran to me. He hugged me, almost suffocating me. My older brother was amazing.

I walked into Bronwyn's house. It was the same as the last time I was here. The piano, the books, the smell of elitism was all here. I carried my bags up the monstrous staircase into my old room. It was still the same. I dropped my luggage. I touched the pillows. The same bedding covered the place that I was able to finally sleep without crying myself to that point. The same paintings hung on the wall. This was my real childhood bedroom. I missed him. He was my real father. He was the one who loved me unconditionally. I gathered my emotions and walked downstairs.

Jackson was in the kitchen preparing our meal. He was as happy to see me as I was happy to see him. We have not gathered for Thanksgiving since our parents died. He was under so much pressure to prepare the perfect reuniting dinner. When Will died, Jackson and I were standing next to each other. Jackson's arm was around my back. His other hand was on Will's body. We were both weeping uncontrollably, but Jackson still held me. Like the perfect big brother, he always took care of me. We talked a few times a week, but we have not seen each other in a few years. His life in Virginia and my life in Atlanta was simply too chaotic to arrange meetings.

It was easier that way for me. It was easier to only connect through the phone to continue to hide my secret.

I walked downstairs and joined Jackson in the kitchen.

Sarah Beth

I WALKED UP TO UNCLE BRONWYN'S HOUSE ECSTATIC because it was the first time that all of the siblings were home for Thanksgiving since our parents' death. We were gathering at Uncle Bronwyn's for dinner and the family tradition of decorating the tree.

I didn't press the doorbell. I grasped the knob and announced my entrance. Gavin and the kids followed me.

I ran to Blake and we hugged for an eternity. I was so happy to see him. He was more muscular than when we saw each other last. I missed him so much. We talked for a few minutes, then he walked over and shook Gavin's hand and started playing with the kids. Joshua loved him.

I walked into the kitchen and stared at Jackson. He was checking the temperature of the turkey. The room smelled like grandmother's Thanksgiving dinner. The smell of pumpkin pie was everywhere. I am not sure where he learned how to make all of this, but in this moment I was reminded of childhood, of mother, and of grandmother. I remembered Will running downstairs stealing dessert and how my grandmother scolded him. He almost started crying. I remember our mother playing the piano while the other adults stood around gossiping about the family.

When he finished checking the turkey, he acknowledged me, and we hugged. I left him in the kitchen and walked through the dining room. Although it was not what I believed in, the table was beautiful. The white china plates were placed perfectly on the chargers, with all of the utensils and Waterford glasses placed perfectly, as our childhood taught us. Aubrey made a cornucopia arrangement that was the perfect centerpiece. The bright autumn colors with small pumpkins and gourds were stunning. I noticed matching mantel pieces. I coveted her attention to detail. The lights glistened through the crystal chandelier that Bronwyn purchased in London. The room was heavenly.

I walked into the parlor and noticed the empty Christmas tree by the front window, with all the tree decorations around the base of the tree. It was always our tradition to decorate the tree after Thanksgiving dinner. In the corner of the room, there were several other boxes of decorations. Then, I realized that Jackson was using all of Bronwyn's decorations. His house always caused Magnolia to become a parking lot because people from miles away would drive over to view his house at Christmas. I was proud that Jackson was reviving the splendor.

I glanced out the front window, and I noticed Blake was playing baseball with all of the kids in the median. Gavin stood by laughing as they played. I was glad Blake was home. I missed him. When he was in high school, Blake came to live with Bronwyn and no one ever spoke of the reason why. It always perplexed me. Our father could be such an ass. When Blake left for

Ole Miss, his visits were sparse. I walked around the house and noticed five other Christmas trees that needed to be decorated.

The doorbell sounded. I walked and opened the door. Aubrey was standing there in a stunning Chanel suit and Jimmy Choo suede pumps. Her pearls draped perfectly around her neck. Her hair was perfectly placed and accented her face and her smile. I enjoyed Aubrey. I welcomed her into the house, and I told her Jackson was in the kitchen, which caused her to want to help him prepare dinner. I was a little happier because I was now free from potential work.

I stepped out onto the porch and watched Abby as she walked up the sidewalk. She was beautiful. She was good for him. They enjoyed each other. Abby was less formal than Aubrey. She wore an Alex Evenings autumn dress. It was fantastic, and she wore it beautifully. It was a light brown color, which she paired with a pair of Chanel wedges. Her pearls were also perfect and matched the pearl bracelet. As she walked up, we both smiled at each other. We hugged, and I walked with her into the house.

As we stood in the kitchen, Ms. Sally walked through the door and into the room. We all loved her. She raised us better than our mother could have. She had a bottle of wine with her, which she placed on the counter. She immediately walked over to the stove and opened the door to examine the turkey. "Well, look at little Jacky. That boy can cook." We all laughed.

I began opening the bottle of wine because it had reached an acceptable hour to do so.

As I twisted the cork, I glanced around and smiled. My family was together. We are here one more time.

Joshua

"DEAR GOD, THANK YOU FOR THE TURKEY AND FOR Uncle Jackson who made it taste so good. Thank you for Uncle Blake and letting him come visit me and show me how to play baseball. Please let me be a baseball player like him. Thank you for my mommy and daddy and my brother and sister. Thank you for Brick and for Faulkner. Thank you for letting them be friends and play together. Thank you for Ms. Aubrey who brought me a present. Thank you for Ms. Abby who plays cards with me. Thank you for Ms. Sally who hugs me so very hard. Thank you for the tree that we get to decorate. Thank you for everything. A-Men."

Aubrey

I WANT TO INTERVENE SO BADLY, BUT IT WOULD BE AS easy as herding cats. They are all just putting each decoration wherever they want, and no one is thinking about how the tree looks. There are places that are crammed with ornaments and places as bare as a baby's bottom. They are not thinking about the color patterns and how the colors should be distributed in an aesthetic manner. This is the tree that the neighbors are going to see. This tree needs a theme. All trees need a theme. Bronwyn would have a theme for each tree in the house.

They are acting like children now. Gavin was the only civil one in the group. He is the only one handing the ornaments to the children and letting them place them on the tree. The other adults are picking up an ornament, putting it on a hook, and placing it on a branch, with no second examination to see if it was the correct spot. This is chaotic. I will fix it tomorrow; they will not know the difference.

Just look at that precious Joshua. He decided he was done with the ornaments. He crawled under the tree. He's just spread out under there smiling, without a care in the world.

Sarah Beth and Gavin have done so well with him. He is such a doll.

Watching the three of them today in the kitchen was so nice. I bet they miss Will. How did Sarah Beth survive childhood growing up with three boys, I will never understand. Hell, that's probably the preparation for the Peace Corps, growing up with the three of those boys.

It was nice to see Abby helping them. I am so glad that Jackson and Abby are dating. They are so perfect for each other. Her patience with Joshua is amazing.

Sarah Beth is so very different than Jackson and Blake. Jackson and Blake were cut from the same cloth, it seemed. Blake has grown into a very handsome young man. I have watched him play ball several times. He is such a strong athlete. I nearly spat out my wine during dinner. We all knew it. But, to hear it come from him in such a casual way brought such laughter from everyone. It was nice. I am glad that he came home.

Oh my. That tree. I just can't stand here and watch that dumpster fire any longer.

As I walked out of the house, I turned left onto Magnolia and walked across the median. The cool air felt refreshing. I walked north for three blocks, passing the Hardings. Shelby was sitting on the porch crying.

"Well, Shelby are you okay honey?"

"Hey Aubrey, Yes, I am fine. Just a little emotional. You know hormones, I guess."

"Okay, honey, do I need to stay for a bit? I don't mind. I am just walking home from Jackson's. Or why don't you come with me?"

"I am fine. Really. We can catch up tomorrow."

I left. We all knew what was wrong with Shelby. I do not understand for the life of me why she stays with him. They have been married long enough for her to receive a decent alimony check. I guess women like that are more afraid of being alone than the abuse of the husband.

I walked one more block and my phone rang. It was Corbin. I answered. He was walking out of the cottage. Poor Shelby. I wish there was something that I could do.

Blake

I AM DRUNK. I MISSED MY FAMILY. I WANT THEM TO know Garrett. He really is a great guy. Dinner was amazing. Jackson did such a great job. There was so much food. I am sitting in the same bed with the same bedding that was here when my father told me to leave. I didn't know where to go. Uncle Bronwyn always knew. He told me I could come here. My father was angry that he offered his home to me, but Bronwyn didn't care. For years, I cried myself to sleep because God didn't love me. He didn't love me, and that broke my heart. As a teen, every night I prayed for God to change me. I prayed for God to do a miracle. I wanted God to love me. I wanted my father to love me, but he stopped. I thought God would stop one day too.

At the lake house, there was a boulder that sat in the side of the back lawn. It had been there for years; no one knew where it came from. As a kid, I would walk to that rock and raise my hand and scream "be moved" because the Bible says that if I had the faith of a mustard seed that I could move mountains. I really believed it. When I was in college, a tornado touched down near the house. There was minimal damage done to the lake house, but the boulder was gone when it was all over. I want to believe that was God showing me that he saw my faith, but it was in his time.

I was a freshman in high school and my best friend was spending the night. We had feelings for each other and were acting out those feelings, when my father opened the door. I was dumb to not have locked it.

My father wanted to send me to conversion camp, but my mother threatened him. I remember hearing her yelling at him about dealing with his sins for years. If he hurt me in any way, she would reveal all of his sins, which he knew would destroy him. I am not sure what those sins were, but he allowed me to live with Uncle Bronwyn for all of my high school years. He rarely spoke to me again because I was an abomination to his family name. I often wondered what was so horrible that he was willing to retreat and listen to my mother. What deep sins had he committed that were worse than my own? I also wondered why my mother stayed with him.

When I graduated from Ole Miss and began to play professional baseball, I was sure that I would never return to this town. I was drafted into the minor leagues, where I played for two years. Afterwards, the Braves wanted me, and I have lived in Atlanta for years. I love baseball, and so did my father. I thought that it would be the bridge to bring us back together, for him to love me regardless of his beliefs. But, it never happened.

I eventually came home to see Uncle Bronwyn, my mother, and Sarah Beth. Family gatherings were always awkward, so I stopped attending them. That's why I was so excited to come home for Thanksgiving. It has been years. Garrett was going to his family, and we decided to tell our families that we were together. I did that this afternoon after Joshua said grace. I said so nonchalantly, "Please pass the mash potatoes, and oh I am gay and have a boyfriend, gravy too please." They all laughed and said, "We know." It finally felt like home.

I knew about Uncle Bronwyn and Boyce. He told me because he saw my pain. He saw that I needed to know that God loved me. I held his secret just as I held my own secret. I wish he was alive now to meet Garrett.

Jackson is playing the piano. Abby and Sarah Beth are singing. I wish I could play. The music reminds me of all of the times we would all gather around the same piano listening to Bronwyn, my mother, and Jackson. They played so well. I was always in awe of them all. Jackson played in a special way. He always seemed to play with a deep rooted emotion; the piano was cathartic for him.

When he told me that he was returning to Culpepper, I was shocked. He swore he would never return to the brick streets of our childhood. He looks great. It is obvious that he is taking care of himself. I was always proud of him. He stood up to our father and refused to go to law school. It was amazing that he was resolute in his choices.

Jackson was playing *How Great Thou Art*. As they sang with him, I remember mother taking us to First Baptist every Sunday. She was so devout. She loved God more deeply than any other person I knew. Her faith was unshakable. She is the reason that I still believe. Because of her, I know that God was guiding my feet. I missed her so much. When we were children, she would gather us in the parlor every evening after dinner. She would read a chapter from the Bible to us. It was part of our nightly ritual, and we were never allowed to miss it.

Sometimes I hated it. But, I missed it so much after I moved in with Bronwyn.

As Jackson played, I remembered one Easter Sunday when Jackson walked downstairs for us to leave for church. He was wearing blue jeans. My mother screamed at him about disrespecting his family by wearing jeans to church on Easter Sunday. We left Jackson at home, but mother demanded that he change and not be late. He walked in and sat on our pew one minute before the service began. That was also the first time that I heard my mother swear. It was time for communion. The usher placed the tray that contained small cups of grape juice into Sarah Beth's hand. She chose her small plastic cup, which contained a little more than a spoonful of grape juice. After choosing her cup, she carefully passed the tray of juice to my mother, who carefully chose her cup of grape juice. As my father took the tray from my mother, Sarah Beth accidently hit mother's other arm and caused mother to spill her cup of juice onto her chest and Easter dress. Before realizing it, my mother whispered, "Shit Sarah Beth" in the quietness of the congregation. An older woman, who was also a deacon's wife, turned slightly around and spoke to mother, "Dear, it happens to all of us. It will be okay." My mother was mortified. We all wanted to laugh, but we knew the consequences of such behavior.

The same deacon's wife calmed my soul so many times. As a child, I discovered a specific sin. When I discovered this sin, I also felt the power of guilt. I felt so horrible afterwards that I would pray for forgiveness and promise God that I would never do it again. But, when the opportunity was available, I sinned again, and the guilt consumed me. Several times, I called that deacon's wife because I needed to know that I was not going to hell. "Mrs. Morris, I have done something horrible. I sinned, and I promised God that I would never do it again. I did it again. Did he forgive me?"

She would always respond, "Blake, God loves you. He forgave you. He loves you so very much. He understands." Then, it would happen again, and I would call Mrs. Morris. Again, she would comfort me and remind me of God's love toward me. I never acknowledged the sin that I continually committed, but I knew that she knew. She was so close to God, that I am sure he told her.

I felt peaceful. My family, the piano, and the memories all comforted me. I lay in the bed listening to their singing. It felt good to be home.

Jackson

I PULLED ALL THE BOXES LABELED "CHRISTMAS" FROM the attic and placed them in the parlor and other first floor rooms last night. Aubrey arrived at nine this morning, the day after Thanksgiving. I was barely awake when the ringing of the doorbell summoned me out of bed. I dressed and allowed her to enter. I am not sure why she was not shopping on Black Friday in Jackson. She stood there completely composed in the most elegant casual attire. She was perfect for a day of decorating the house, which I despised doing. She held her Ole Miss coffee cup in her right hand, and in a quiet southern voice, she asked if she woke me. I responded appropriately, and she followed me into the parlor. A radiant smile encompassed her face. That is when I knew she was the perfect person for the job. I placed four hundred dollars into her pocket, and retreated to the coffee pot that was calling my name. She followed me, demanding that she was not going to take the money.

I made my regular breakfast, a bowl of warm oatmeal and my first cup of coffee with heavy cream, while listening to Aubrey sing along with the music on her phone. When I had finished the bowl, I carried my coffee into the hallway. I glanced into the parlor. Aubrey was dancing, her hips swinging back and forth as she carefully noted each box's contents. I returned to my bedroom to read the morning paper.

It was 10:30 when I left my room, ready for a morning run and to escape the chaos of Uncle Bronwyn's house. I chose to be away all day.

As I walked out of the house, I turned north on Magnolia. It was a warm Black Friday, and I wanted to feel the breeze off the river. When I reached the commercial area of Magnolia, I turned left and ran toward the river. When I reached the river walk, I stopped to admire the powerful force of nature. The river was sometimes a scary place. As children we were all told to never play in the river. Every year, several people drown in her currents. There were warning signs for miles along the banks, but people simply believed that they were stronger than the currents. I ran beside her. I muted my music. There were no boats, but the waves were fierce. The rain over the past few days had invigorated her. She ran beside me flexing her might for me. I ran listening to her power. It made me run faster.

As I ran, I realized that I could not run from being a Kensington. I was still the son of a man who raped Ms. Sally. I was the grandson of a racist who pulled men off buses and burnt them with torches. In the chaos of my mind, I made the connection. My father learned his behavior from his father. I questioned my own life. I ran faster. What if I were a racist too? What if the daily actions of my classroom were racist, and I was not aware. My mind flashed back for years attempting to recognize any racist moments that existed in my own life. What lives in my college classroom had I cursed? I ran questioning the past.

Then, suddenly I found myself slowing down. The waves seemed to calm some. The wide river walk had narrowed and was now surrounded by trees and grass. The solid cement pathway no longer existed. There was no longer a wall separating me from the river as she flowed peacefully seven feet away. We were only separated by green grass. The birds were loud. I began to jog, matching her rhythm.

After running, I showered at Abby's. When I was done, we joined Blake and walked north on Magnolia to find lunch. As we walked, I held Abby's hand. Her soft skin rubbing against my palms. We noticed that I was not the only neighbor who chose to decorate on black Friday. We settled for a café on First Avenue.

The three of us sat at a table on the sidewalk. It was a beautiful November morning. We all abhorred shopping, especially on crazy days such as today. We wanted to enjoy the vacancy of the city. As we sat there, I glanced into Abby's eyes. I wanted to ask her about our future. I wanted to know where we were going. I was planning to return to Virginia, and she was going back to Charleston.

As I stared at her, Blake punched me in the arm. He wanted me to see an old drunk man stumbling near us on the sidewalk. I glanced over, and I saw Whit. I stood up and walked to him. I touched his shoulder and invited him to sit with us. He refused. I patted him on his shoulder and wished him a good day.

When Blake and I returned to the house, I was stunned to see how quickly the house was transformed. The wreaths were on all the outside windows. She had collected fresh garland to cover the iron fence that covered the perimeter of the lawn. As I walked into the foyer, I noticed, she placed a poinsettia on opposite sides of every third step on the stairway. Fresh garland was wrapped around each banister. The placement of each red, gold, and white bow was precise and purposeful. Each mantel on the first floor had fresh garland and Christmas candles, with bows that matched the tree in the room. The Christmas village, which consisted of replicas of the houses in the historic district, was placed on the buffet in the parlor. As I walked to view each tree, I noticed each tree maintained a theme. They were beautiful. Even the tree in the parlor seemed more beautiful than it did the night before. The one in the parlor now contained a handmade bow constructed with wide white and silver ribbon that extended vertically the length of the tree. The tree in the dining room matched the colors in the china. The tree in the library was decorated in darker hues of red and deep golden colors. The ribbon was a deep crimson with sporadic golden spots. The ribbon was wrapped around the tree in a diagonal pattern. At the top of the tree, Aubrey had placed a golden angel. There was also a tree on the sun porch that was decorated in an SEC theme. All of the colors of the SEC were represented.

The dining room table was exquisite. My great grandmother's Christmas china was placed perfectly on the table; the centerpiece was a stunning collection of fresh garland, cranberry candles, and white blossoms. The house smelled of cinnamon. I am not sure how Aubrey had created the homemade smell, but it complemented the beauty of the house.

The house was perfect.

Michael

GOOD MORNING, AND WELCOME TO FIRST BAPTIST. WE
are so glad that you are with us today. I am going to do something a little out of the ordinary this morning. Don't worry, we
will still be out of here by noon. This is the Sunday after Thanksgiving. In most churches across the country, the sermon from
the pulpit will include the notions of being thankful. Normally,
I would deliver such a sermon. But, this morning, I feel that God
wants to lead us down a different path.

Yesterday was a hot Mississippi Saturday. In the afternoon, I
decided to walk on the river walk, so that I could reflect on this
morning's service. I felt a special need to spend time with God,
searching for the truth that he wanted me to share this morning.
As I walked lost in the peace of the river and the breeze, I noticed a man, a woman, and a small child about 70 feet in front of
me. As I walked closer, I noticed the child was crouched down
on the river walk and attempted to pick up something. I was curious. When I was close enough, I realized that it was Gavin and
Sarah Beth with their son, Joshua. Mom and Dad were standing
and watching Joshua pick up a worm and walk to the other side

185

of the river walk. He, then, walked into the grass and dug a small trench in the dirt with his finger. Carefully, he placed the worm into the small trench and moved grass on top of the trench for protection.

I want you to truly visualize what Joshua was doing. I want you all to have the image of a little boy picking up a worm and taking the worm to the grass. He did it in such a precise and well planned manner. He was methodical.

When he had completed his task, I looked at him. "Joshua what you doing?" He replied, "I was helping that worm get to the other side of the road." I paused for a moment. "Why would you do that?" I asked. He began to explain that the pavement was hot. It was a long way for the worm to crawl. He said, "If I don't help the worm, he will fry because it's so hot." He continued to explain to me that the worm needed to get to that grass for a reason. Joshua didn't understand what that reason was. He explained to me that maybe, the worm wanted to visit his mommy and daddy. Or maybe, the worm wanted to see his brothers and sisters. No matter the reason, the worm needed to get to the grass.

And then, Joshua said one of the most profound things I have heard in a long time. "Mr. Michael, the worm needed my help. So, I helped him." And, then Joshua shrugged his shoulders and started skipping down the river walk.

I looked at Gavin and Sarah Beth and smiled. As I walked away, I began to cry. In that moment, God used the innocence of a child to remind me of the purpose of humanity. I want to return to the scripture that we read several weeks ago.

If you have your Bible, please follow along: Matthew 22: 34-40. But when the Pharisees had heard that he had put the

Sadducees to silence, they were gathered together. Then one of them, which was a lawyer, asked him a question, tempting him, and saying, Master, which is the great commandment in the law? Jesus said unto him, Thou shalt love the Lord thy God with all thy heart, and with all thy soul, and with all thy mind. This is the first and great commandment. And the second is like unto it, Thou shalt love thy neighbor as thyself.

Here, we learn of the command to love our neighbor as we love ourselves. It was not a suggestion, but rather, it is a command. We must love God first, and then our neighbors.

If we continue to search the scriptures, there are numerous other passages that command us to love others. We are commanded to care for the poor and the sick. We are commanded to love others as Christ loves them.

Joshua could have skipped over that worm. But, instead he stopped in his busy afternoon. He did not see a piece of fish bait. He did not see a crawling creature. He saw someone who had a mommy and daddy; he saw the humanity of the situation. He knew that it was his job to help the worm because he knew the hot sun would bake the worm on the black asphalt river walk.

Some of the greatest lessons come from the most innocent around us.

Sometimes in my life, there have been moments when I was the worm. I was a poor college student working part time at the Baptist Campus Ministries office at Ole Miss. There was one time when I was not able to pay my rent. My parents and grandparents could not help. I was upset one evening, completely worried that God was not going to help me out. As I sat on the bench in front of the dining hall, a professor walked by me. He knew I was upset. He asked if he could sit down beside me.

187

We talked, and I expressed my fears. He took my hand, and he prayed for me right there on the bench outside of the dining hall. He did not know me.

The next day someone paid my rent. I never found out who did it. Perhaps, it was the professor. But in that moment, he was my Joshua, a stranger stopping by on a hot sunny day, helping me cross the path to get to get the grass.

Later, I took an English class, and he walked into the room. I knew he remembered me, as I did him.

In this chaotic world, we are so busy working. We rarely put our phones down. We rarely fully engage in other's lives. We ignore the homeless man on Third Avenue because he smells. We avoid certain parts of town because of the people who live there. We don't engage with our neighbors.

In the ignoring, the avoidance, and the disengagement, we are missing opportunities to love our neighbors. We are missing the moments to help someone in need. We are missing the moments to be Joshua to someone.

Joshua was simply going through his day, skipping down the river walk with his parents. Suddenly, he saw someone in need. Joshua didn't know the worm. But, Joshua knew that without his help the worm would not survive. He knew he was meant to help.

We all need a heart like Joshua. His heart is a heart of service and love. He did not ask a series of questions to see if the worm was worthy of help. He did not care about the worm's ethnicity, whether it was an earth worm or some other type of worm. He did not care about the circumstances that caused the worm to be on the hot asphalt. All Joshua saw was someone who needed his help.

I want us to notice something else about Joshua. He did not place the worm in the trench, and wait for the worm to say, "Thanks, Joshua." He placed the worm in the trench, and then went further by providing additional protection from the heat. Then, he stood and continued about his day, expecting nothing in return. He did not look at his parents and wait for a "that a boy" or a "great job." He did not look at his pastor for praise.

As we end this service this morning, I want you to remember that there are people sitting in this church who are struggling in ways that you will never understand. Your neighbors are good at hiding their pain. They are good at hiding their problems. As you leave this morning, please find a way to be a Joshua to someone this week. We must love people where they are, as God commands us to do.

Please stand if you are able. The doors of the church are open if you feel God is leading you to become part of this church family.

Eric

JACKSON'S HOUSE LOOKED AMAZING. AS WE WALKED across the median, I fully noticed the beauty of Christmas. I held Emily's moist hand. I could tell Emily was nervous, but she was not willing to stay away from one of the most important Christmas parties of the year. She and I had already had a bottle of wine to help us through the evening.

As we approached the door, a butler waited patiently for our coats. As we walked in, I quickly scanned the room to locate a beverage. I placed my hand in the small of Emily's back, and we made our way into the parlor, where there was a bartender. I walked toward him to retrieve two glasses of red wine. Emily walked toward Elizabeth and Patrick Hathaway.

I collected our glasses and returned to Emily. As they chatted, I noticed the large number of people in the house. I noticed a server walking through the crowds with hors d'oeuvres. I stopped him and gathered some food. Emily completed her conversation with Elizabeth, and we continued through the crowd. Jackson and Abby were in the kitchen chatting with

190

Victoria, Auden, and a state congressman who lived in Jackson. We walked over apprehensively.

Everyone exchanged salutations. Victoria was completely cordial with Emily. Indeed, she is southern, so I was not surprised.

I walked to a second bar in the kitchen to refill my wine glass. Everyone who lives in the district seemed to be here tonight. As I glanced around, I noticed the true formality of the evening. Jackson revealed the truest level of his elitism. All of the staff were in black tuxedos. There were numerous flower arrangements in every room. Each arrangement matched the Christmas trees that Aubrey created. The men were all wearing coats and ties, most in tuxedos. Most of the women wore an evening gown. I was amazed at the beauty of it all.

Emily was talking to the governor. I contemplated saving him from her ramblings, but instead, I wanted a cigarette. I retreated to the back lawn.

There were several smokers among Culpepper's citizens, so I felt that it was appropriate to partake as well. Though, a blunt would be much more enjoyable at this time in my life. There were several of us in the district that gathered on occasion to enjoy our special cigarettes, but this was not one of those occasions.

I stood there and watched as my neighbors engaged with each other. I wondered how many of them knew. I wonder how many of them actually cared. My life was falling apart around me. I can't tell Emily. I can't. It would crush her. It crushes me. They all have to know that I can't take care of my family.

The nicotine rushed through my blood. It comforted me. It calmed me.

Auden

ERIC WAS INCREDIBLY INEBRIATED TONIGHT. WE WERE standing in the backyard chatting as he smoked a cigarette. I asked about his house and the repairs and questioned why it was taking so long. He started tearing up. I could see the stress appear on his face. Eric began to explain to me that he was in financial distress. The business entered a rough time, and Eric stopped paying the home insurance. The fire caused thousands of dollars in damage, mainly to the front of the second story. He had spent the last few weeks attempting to complete the repairs himself, but it was becoming overwhelming.

As we stood there with tears running down his face, I sympathized with him. He was a father trying to care for his family. I touched his shoulder and grasped it firmly to make him look at me. I told him that I would have my contractor stop by his house next week. I would pay for the repairs, and he can pay me back when he settled on his feet again. The tears increased. We shook hands, and I walked away, so he could compose himself.

Abby

THE PARTY WAS WONDERFUL. JACKSON WAS THE PER-
fect host. I was amazed at how well it was turning out. The governor tempted Jackson to play the piano. He wanted to hear
Christmas carols. Others began coaxing Jackson to play. He
glanced at me. I nodded my head approvingly. He walked over
to the Steinway, and pretended to push back the fake tails of
his tuxedo that he was not wearing. They laughed. He sat. He
began playing "Silent Night" and the crowd standing in the parlor grew. People began singing. The chorus of revelers sounded
amazing. There must have been thirty or more people gathered
in the parlor singing. Next, Jackson asked Sarah Beth to join
him at the piano. He began playing "O Holy Night," and Sarah
Beth started to sing. Her voice was angelic. There were several
women who gasped. As she sang, the angels stopped to listen
to her. From there, Jackson played seven or eight other Christmas carols with the crowd singing, as more and more people
attempted to enter the parlor.

Jackson

THE PARTY WAS FANTASTIC. THE NEXT MORNING I RE-
turned to the attic because the attic engendered my writing.
There were secrets buried in it, secrets that I wanted to know. As
I rummaged through more of the boxes, I noticed a box with a
scripted M marking its outside. I pulled the box from the highest
shelf. Cautiously, I opened the lid and noticed hundreds of newspaper clippings. "Victoria Harrington Appointed Federal Judge",
"Governor Signs Bill 3506 into Law", and "Lt. Governor Assassinated" among hundreds of other clippings. In the midst of the
clippings, there were pictures of me graduating from Alabama,
two of the photographs were my hooding ceremony and one
depicted my family and me. I was confused. The doorbell rang.
Blake was home for Christmas. I returned the box to the shelf,
closed and locked the door, and ran downstairs to meet him.

Blake arrived the morning of our family dinner to celebrate
Christmas, which Sarah Beth was hosting. As they walked in,
Blake introduced Garrett. We chatted for a few moments, and
they retreated to the cottage, where they were staying for a few
days.

Around two in the afternoon, we walked up the driveway leading to Sarah Beth's home. Blake and Garrett walked slowly behind me. As we walked over, Brick ran at full speed toward us, with slobber slinging right and left from his mouth. He was a beautiful black lab; he and Faulkner were best friends. The slobber met my khakis and the wetness permeated to my skin.

We walked up the steps onto the porch. My hand reached for the door, when Joshua flung it open. He was excited. He hugged me, and then ran down the long hallway that divided the home. He called my name from his bedroom. His bed was covered in gifts from Santa. His face illuminated with the most innocent smile. I sat on the bed as he showed me his toys.

After a few minutes, Sarah Beth summoned me into the kitchen. She and Garrett were drinking a Sam Adams winter lager. They were arguing about some minute detail of a Williams play, which seemed odd because my sister fancied herself a Tennessee Williams scholar. I reached for a beer. As the dark brown liquid rolled down my throat, a chill filled my chest. The smell of the beer reminded me of Will and his love for craft beer. I wish he were here.

As I stood at the counter watching Sarah Beth complete dinner preparations, I glanced through the window and noticed Gavin outside playing basketball with Joseph. Gavin raised his arms and shot the ball. Joseph jumped vertically, and with his right hand blocked the ball, denying it access to the net. He landed squarely on his feet and began laughing because he stole his father's victory. Gavin grabbed his son, and they began roughhousing. Gavin was a wonderful father.

Dinner smelled amazing. Sarah Beth was a wonderful chef. She opened the oven and removed a pan of biscuits. The aroma filled my nostrils. My mother made the best biscuits, ones that we could never replicate no matter how hard we tried. As a child, I would run downstairs almost every Saturday morning to fresh biscuits. I would slice one open and swipe the butter into both halves. As the butter melted carelessly, I would apply the perfect amount of maple syrup or pear preserves to each side of the biscuit. I had to wait for the appropriate amount of time for each side to absorb the liquids.

My mother was an excellent cook, but she was also an excellent southerner. Every year, she would spend hours making every type of preserve known to man. The basement shelves were inundated with each type of preserve, perfectly labeled. When she died, we all took solace in the preserves that she left for us. But, there was always that entrenched feeling of knowing that one day there will only be one jar left, one lonely jar of remembrance with which we would have to deal. We could never replicate her preserves, and the last jar would remind us of our loss, knowing that the last thing that she made for us was also leaving. We needed that remembrance. We could not let the last piece of love from our mother drift into eternity. In the basement of the house, there is one jar for each of us to always have.

The clanking of Julia's heels on the hardwood floors abruptly jarred me from my memory. Julia was sixteen years old, Sarah Beth's oldest. Sarah Beth's voice called Julia and the rest of us to the table.

Sarah Beth's home was one of the larger houses on First Avenue. Sarah Beth seemed to rebel against the traditional values of southern culture. There was not a piano in the parlor, indeed, there was not a parlor in the house. Sarah Beth demolished the wall separating the parlor from the library to create a larger room, which became the gathering space for the family. There was a large television mounted over the fireplace, a large hunter green leather sectional placed in the center of the room. She also removed the wall that divided the kitchen from the dining room, to create a larger open space on that side of the house. There was a staircase in the kitchen that led to the back of the second floor, and another staircase in the foyer that ended in the front of the second floor.

We gathered in the dining space. There were no name plates to give seating directions. The dinner plates were on the light gray and white granite countertop that matched the gray cabinets. We were instructed to form a line, fill our plates, and sit where we wanted. The lack of formality annoyed me, but to Sarah Beth such formality was always superfluous and divisive.

As we ate, we began discussing childhood memories. Sarah Beth reminded us of the time we tricked Will into allowing us to bury him in the backyard at the lake house. He was an incredibly intelligent person, but sometimes common sense was not his strongest attribute. We dug a hole, and Will lay in the trench while we piled the dirt on top of him. The three of us simply ran away, leaving him trapped in the earth. Mother had to threaten to beat us before we provided Will's escape.

I glanced at everyone. The laughter and the joy comforted me. We were home.

Ms. Sally

I HAD TO EXCUSE MYSELF FOR A MINUTE FROM THE table. I needed some air. I raised those kids in that room. I spanked them when they were bad. I wiped their noses when they were sick. I have so many memories of those kids. I never thought that I would ever see this day. They are all here. All of them but Will. He is here, though. I know he is. I am so proud of all of them. When their mother died, I knew I would never see them all together again. I just knew it would never happen. I thought Thanksgiving was a touch from God to get them together, but now to see it a second time. I am in awe of God's grace. I see the hand of God on my family. I know Ms. Elizabeth would be proud of them too.

Abby

JACKSON AND I STOOD IN THE HATHAWAY'S HOME with the rest of our neighborhood friends. We held our champagne waiting for the television to display the dropping of the ball in Times Square. Shelby and Matthew were standing together by the fireplace. Auden and Victoria were standing beside us. Patrick was holding Elizabeth's hand. They were such a beautiful couple. The years of love written on both of their faces. Sarah Beth was sitting in the Queen Anne chair and Gavin stood behind her with his hands on her shoulders. Corbin, Cara, and Aubrey were sitting on the sofa. All of us staring and counting toward a new year in the district.

Phoebe

IT WAS COLD OUT THIS MORNING. AS I REACHED DOWN to pick up the paper, I noticed Whit was staggering north through the median. I began to chuckle.

I turned toward my house and walked a few steps while unfolding it to the front page. "The Hattiesburg Stocking Strangler Is Coming to Culpepper" was the headline. According to the paper, the case has been moved from Hattiesburg to Culpepper and Auden Harrington is the defendant's attorney. Auden loved the spotlight and the national attention. The case was beginning in three weeks, and everyone should expect high traffic and the national media in downtown Culpepper.

I glanced up and saw Jackson. He smiled and walked over. We chatted for a few minutes, and he left running north on the street. I have never known anyone who ran as much as he did. As I opened the door, Corbin was walking out the side door.

Auden

I WOKE UP THIS MORNING THINKING ABOUT BOYCE. I missed him. As I walked to my office, I remembered his intelligence. He would argue with a fence post in the most intellectual discourse. He would have been an accomplished attorney.

What is Whit doing in the median? That man is always drunk.

As I walked through the district, I realized how destructive this place truly could be. My heart ached. When we were younger, Victoria and I loved living here. As we have aged, we have seen the district detach itself from so many. I am convinced that Boyce gave up and died because he was alone, left to die alone by the numerous neighbors whom he called friends. They abandoned him.

The air was warm for an early February morning. The sun rested in a cloudless bright sky. I was going to my office and then to court. The murder trial begins this morning.

I know my client did not commit these murders, and it is my job to prove his innocence. Jason Cortez lived outside of Hattiesburg, and he was a cook and a server at the Club of

Hattiesburg, a prestigious private dinner club. According to the district attorney, Jason befriended a number of the older wealthy women who were members of the club. He would chat with them extensively when they were in the club for dinner. He knew when the women were home alone. At the precise time, Jason broke into the homes, murdered the women and stole as much as he could. In total, three women were killed and over a million dollars of property was stolen and sold.

Jason denied committing the crimes. Jason's family was not able to pay my fees, but another benefactor will cover the costs. I asked the judge to move the case to Culpepper because everyone in Hattiesburg knows of Jason and the women who were murdered. I argued he would receive a more fair trial two hours away in a small town. I was not shocked when Judge Carmichael moved the case.

Whit

THE SUN RAYS FALL ON US. IT IS SAFE HERE. CAN YOU hear me? The sun upon our faces. Dance with me. Laugh with me. Sing with me. The sun. The grass. The wind. Know me. Know me well. Sing. Dance. Laugh with me in the grass.

Jackson

I WALKED OVER TO PICK ABBY UP SO THAT WE COULD walk to dinner. February in Mississippi can be a strange month. But, on this particular evening, the sky was clear and the temperature was perfect. She caressed my hand with her fingers as we walked up the sidewalk. She was telling me about her day, and to be honest, my mind was somewhere else. I was still attempting to frame the words that I would use later. I smiled and laughed when appropriate, but I was not completely focused on her.

At seven, we arrived at the Cellar, and sat at the bar. Matt gave us menus and explained the evening specials. Abby noticed that several of our friends from the historic district were also out to dinner.

I ordered a Hillrock, and she decided that she wanted one too. I enjoyed her. I loved her intelligence and her love for humanity. Her kindness was amazing. She was driven and full of dreams. As we ate, we chatted about our work weeks, and I genuinely listened. Occasionally, one of our friends stopped by and chatted with us for a few minutes. It was nice to have such a nice neighborhood.

Matt walked over and asked if we needed anything else. I looked at Abby. I took her hand. She looked at me strangely.

"Abby, I met you in this exact spot seven months ago to this day. You walked in here and you had a choice of two seats, both on either side of me. I don't think you really had a choice of not meeting me. Over these months, you have challenged me to be a better person. You have challenged me to reach for my greatest potential. Abby, I have fallen in love with you. I know it has been a short time. I know that I live in Virginia and you live in Charleston. But, I also know that I do not want to spend the rest of my life wondering 'what if?' I am not saying let's do it tomorrow or next month, or even within a year. All I am saying is that I love you, and I do not want to miss the chance to have you for the rest of my life. Abby, will you marry me?"

Matt produced the three carat emerald cut diamond ring that I had given to the owner earlier in the day.

Abby said yes, and the restaurant all clapped and shouted. I placed the ring on her finger, and I kissed her.

"Thank you for making me so very happy."

The blinds were lowered. A sign was placed on the door that read "Private Party," and the rest of our friends came from the back of the restaurant. I had reserved the entire restaurant to celebrate our engagement with our friends from the historic district.

Blake walked around the corner and hugged me. I was so glad that my best man could come for the occasion.

After the engagement, I walked Abby home. As we were walking, the clouds opened and large drops of rain began falling upon us. We did not care. We did not walk faster. We stopped, and I kissed her under the drops that fell from the large magnolia

205

leaves that protected us. As I held her, I realized that I had made the right decision.

The next day was a normal day of chores around the house, and preparing for our trip to Jackson to celebrate our engagement. My mother raised us to enjoy the arts, and we spent a great deal of time engaged in artistic events throughout the south. The night after our engagement party, I took Abby to the Grand Opera House in Jackson. It is an enormous and beautiful structure that was built in 1890. My favorite opera, Puccini's *La bohème*, was opening, and I wanted her to experience the greatest love story of all time. It is the story of two people in extreme poverty who fall in love and fight those attractions. In the end, the couple reunite, and Mimi dies in her lover's arms because of an illness.

As the opera ended, tears could be heard throughout the massive structure. The greatest of southern men, like the governor who sat three seats from us, cried like babies. I always loved the impact of the opera on others' souls. If we allow each aspect of the experience to enter into our lives, the influence can be monumental. It's what my mother loved about the opera. It is why this opera was being performed in the hall named Elizabeth Kensington Hall. My mother served on the board of directors for twenty years total. When the hall needed repairs, Elizabeth Bradford Kensington paid for the repairs. She believed in the aesthetic experience that only the opera can give to someone.

It was Abby's first time. She cried more than I did, which surprised me. As our driver picked us up, Abby was still crying. We sat in the back seat of the Lincoln discussing the events of the evening all the way home.

After the opera, we met Victoria, Auden, Elizabeth, and

Patrick for drinks at the Hathaway's house. Elizabeth Hathaway was the replication of every ideal of southern culture. Her voice reminded me of sweet tea and southern values. She was the epitome of a perfect southern woman. Her home was also the representation of a true southern home. A few years ago, her home was photographed for Southern Living magazine. There is a picture of Elizabeth and Patrick standing in front of the massive mahogany staircase, with the American foxhound puppy in the background. The photograph was her inspiration for the oil painting that hangs over the marble fireplace in the parlor.

I consider myself southern, but being in her presence sometimes intimidated me. She was the only woman who could destroy someone's self-esteem while maintaining the most precise southern smile and southern warmness. She was by far one of my favorite citizens of the historic district.

As we sat in the Hathaway's living room, I glanced at Abby. Her blue eyes were radiant. Her smile was sincere. She caught me staring. Her smile became an obvious corrective glare. She did not want me to draw attention, though they all knew that I was enamored by her.

After an appropriate amount of time with the group, Auden and Victoria stood to excuse themselves; Abby and I did the same. It was an enjoyable evening for everyone. I loved these evenings because I could sit and listen to the inner workings of the district.

When we left the Hathaway's home, we walked south on Magnolia to Uncle Bronwyn's house. I wanted to give Faulkner some outdoor time before walking Abby home.

As I was leaving Abby's, I could feel a coldness in the air. The damp night air was refreshing. I walked slowly north on

Magnolia. I walked past Uncle Bronwyn's house, still enjoying the air. As I neared where Boyce lived, I stared into the large open window. A new family had purchased the home. He was a young Captain in the Army with a new wife and a new baby. It was nice that the loneliness had been replaced with happiness.

I walked slowly north when I heard noises coming from the next block. I began to run to the chaos. The older man was laying on the sidewalk begging for the man to stop, but Matthew was not hindered by his words. Matthew Harding was kicking the older gentleman and yelling with each kick. "Find somewhere else to sleep. Stay off my lawn." I ran faster. As I shoved Matthew, I could smell the alcohol swimming from his pores. I reached down to the old man. It was Whit. The tears from his eyes shared the pain within his heart. I picked him up and carried him toward Uncle Bronwyn's.

Whit was also slightly inebriated. We walked into the median and followed the median south, until we were in front of Uncle Bronwyn's house. He refused to leave the median. He rambled about the green grass and the safety of the grass. We laid in the grass and stared upward into the clear cold sky. The stars radiated a peaceful glow that captured me. It grabbed me and would not release me. I chose not to fight. I simply stared into the clearness of it all. I am not sure why but in that moment the photographs of my grandfather were no longer burdening my soul. For months, the pain chained me. I was angry. I hated him and what he did to those people. The secrets of the man that I loved so dearly tethered me. Laying in the grass staring into the beauty of the light in the darkness removed his dead albatross from my neck.

I heard the pastor who baptized me when I was 12 call my

name aloud. "Dr. Jackson Kensington will deliver today's message." I stood from the first pew, and I walked slowly to the pulpit. I was dressed in my regalia. The dark blue velvet was a testament of my perseverance. It was Easter Sunday, and each pew was packed to capacity. I glanced over the congregation. On the seventh pew on the right side of the church, Big Daddy sat beside Big Momma holding her hand. My parents sat next to them; his left arm rested on the top of the pew behind mother's neck. His huge hand grasping the top of the pew, as if he was holding on for a reason. Will sat on the right of Sarah Beth and Gavin. Joshua sat on the floor under the pew at his parents' feet. Blake was between our parents and Will.

I stood there staring at all of them. I opened my bible, and I stepped to the right of the pulpit. The bible rested in my left hand. I began to read the story of the woman who walked over to Jesus as he was eating at Simon's home. She sat at Jesus' feet and began to weep. She anointed his feet with oil and wiped them with her hair while she kissed them. Suddenly, my regalia was absent, and I stood in front of everyone completely naked. As my words entered the congregation, the doors of the sanctuary opened, and Ms. Sally walked into the service. She was stunningly beautiful. Her hat and gloves were perfect. She walked down the aisle and sat beside Blake, who hugged her and kissed her cheek as she sat down. Mother reached over Blake and grasped her hand. She held it, not wanting to let it go. We loved her. I loved her. I stood naked in front of all of them.

As the sun rose the next morning, I opened my eyes to find Joshua standing over me. He was laughing at me. Sarah Beth stood with a sheer look of worry on her face. Whit was gone. I raised my upper body from the grass, and Joshua sat in my lap.

The dream was still present in my mind. Sarah Beth sat next to us. She began laughing. I began laughing. Joshua jumped up and began laughing, skipping, and singing. He ran frantically in circles around us, laughing and pointing at us. He stopped, clutched handfuls of green grass and threw them on me. The blades floated through the air and landed peacefully on me.

Joshua

UNCLE JACKSON IS ASLEEP IN THE GRASS. HE IS DREAM-
ing. His eyes are moving. He looks silly. Uncle Jackson is sleeping in the grass. I know why. I sleep in the grass too. I know why
Uncle Jackson is asleep in the grass. I know why. Right. Right.
Right. Right. The grass needs to fall on him like the rain. Right.
Right. Right. Right. I am going to make it rain grass. Grass falling. Right. Right. Right. Right.

Michael

GOOD MORING. WELCOME TO FIRST BAPTIST CHURCH.
We are so excited that you are here today. Hallelujah He is Ris-
en! He is Risen Indeed! If you have your bible please turn to
John 20:24-29. Now Thomas (also known as Didymus), one of
the Twelve, was not with the disciples when Jesus came. So the
other disciples told him, "We have seen the Lord!" But he said
to them, "Unless I see the nail marks in his hands and put my
finger where the nails were, and put my hand into his side, I will
not believe." A week later his disciples were in the house again,
and Thomas was with them. Though the doors were locked, Jesus
came and stood among them and said, "Peace be with you!" Then
he said to Thomas, "Put your finger here; see my hands. Reach
out your hand and put it into my side. Stop doubting and believe." Thomas said to him, "My Lord and my God!" Then Jesus
told him, "Because you have seen me, you have believed; blessed
are those who have not seen and yet have believed."

This Easter Sunday I want us to view the story of Easter
from a different lens. Through the years, a number of Christians
have thought that this story was just about Thomas. It was about

him and his faith. Perhaps, we want to focus on it this way because of our own connection to doubt. In many ways, we see ourselves attempting to find faith and to truly believe in Jesus and a risen savior.

But, let's pause for a moment and examine what Thomas is focused on. He is focused on the wounded Jesus. Thomas knew what to look for. Anyone who claimed to be the risen Christ must have the wounds that Jesus suffered during his crucifixion. Thomas knew that Jesus would have wounds.

Perhaps it was because Thomas had pain in his own life. He knew what real pain was.

Resurrection does not mean that the pain and the wounds of the crucifixion never happened. Resurrection does not mean that people never mocked our Lord. Resurrection does not mean that a soldier never pierced Christ's side. Resurrection doesn't pretend that the darkness never happened. Rather, it finds a way to focus on the light through the darkness.

It would be nice to forget the wounds. It would be nice to only focus on the joy of it all. But, we can't celebrate the power of resurrection unless we realize that it is all part of the Easter Story.

The disciples ran to Thomas and said, "We have seen Jesus." Thomas replied, "Unless I see and touch the wounds, I won't believe." Thomas knew the wounded Jesus. The only savior strong enough to bare the pain of all of our wounds is a savior who has an intimate knowledge of a wounded self. Christ understands our wounds because he experienced wounds. That is a powerful statement.

We all have wounds. Some of our wounds we have carried for years. Some of our wounds seem unbearable any longer.

Perhaps on this Easter Sunday, you are wounded. Perhaps beneath the new clothes and hats, beneath the pearls and smiles, perhaps there are wounds. Wounds from years ago. Wounds that simply seem to never heal. I challenge you to let the wounded Jesus heal them all.

Please stand if you are able. The doors of the church are open if you feel God is leading you to become part of this church family.

Aubrey

IT WAS A WARM SPRING MORNING. I PULLED THE SIDE door of First Baptist opened. Michael was standing in his office door waiting for me. The tears were already flowing down my face. He hugged me. The tears became more apparent. The pain of my college days was merging with the pain from a few months ago.

We walked into his office, and he closed the door. I sat on the left side of the sofa. He rested in a deep brown leather chair across from me. He offered me tea. I refused. His face was the most caring face I have ever seen. I told him. I told him everything. I have never shared with anyone about the night in the college fraternity house at Ole Miss, and what I did afterward. I have never told anyone that I killed Boyce.

He stood and walked over to the sofa. He sat beside me and placed a box of tissues in my hand. He held me. His embrace was the most important thing that could have happened. He simply held me. There was no judgement. No words of condemnation. He simply held my heart in his arms.

After a few moments, he slid slightly to his left and turned toward me. I faced him. He took my hands and held them. As he prayed for me, I was crying uncontrollably. Years of guilt were leaving my soul. I was never good enough for God. I was never good enough to live. I was a horrible human walking around making decisions about who should be given a chance to live.

After his prayer, he returned to his former position. He held me. I sobbed. He simply held me.

Abby

APRIL 22 IS A DAY I WILL ALWAYS REMEMBER. I TOLD Jackson that I had meetings in Tupelo and would be away for a few days. The drive to Jackson only lasted forty-five minutes. I pulled into the parking space slowly and deliberately. The warmer spring air slapped my face as I exited the vehicle. Assuredly, I walked toward the office door. I pulled the handle and walked over to the counter to check in with the receptionist. I wrote my name as quickly as I could on the sign-in sheet. This was my second visit. She smiled, and we exchanged brief salutations. I sat in the chair waiting for my turn to enter through the doors.

Jackson

I WOKE THIS MORNING AND COMPLETED MY NORMAL routine. Abby was on her way to Tupelo for a business meeting, so I was alone for most of the day.

After dinner, I decided to return to the attic. The boxes glared at me. Bronwyn was incredibly meticulous about everything in life. His attention to detail amazed me. I missed him. I missed how he played the piano. His fingers glided over the keys as if he was David playing his harp. He played with such purpose. He was my inspiration to play, and I wanted to play in the same manner.

I glanced around the room, and I noticed the broom that I brought upstairs with me earlier in the week. I picked it up, and moved around the room moving the broom in a left to right motion. As I swept the floor, I noticed something was on the floor in the bottom right corner of the wall of boxes. It was pushed back closer to the wall. I lay on the floor to retrieve the box. It was smaller than the others, which allowed it to be hidden. The box was labeled, "Jackson." I felt uneasy. I opened the box to find an envelope with my name inscribed on it. I paused and wondered about the contents. I was scared. All of the information that Bronwyn collected in this attic was painful for me. I stood there holding a letter that I was certain would continue those emotions. Did I really want to know its contents? What horrible items had he collected about me? My mind raced through my history. I was certain. I broke the seal and found a letter. It was a handwritten letter on Bronwyn's stationery.

Dearest Jackson,

If you are reading this, then my soul has left this world, and you have returned to the district. I chose you because I believe that you will honor my last wish.

This envelope contains a key to a locked door in the attic. The locked door opens into a closet. I have placed the only key to the closet in this envelope. In the closet, there are boxes that are labeled with specific names on the boxes. Please do not open the boxes. Please deliver each box to its recipient. There is a box for your mother and your father. You may open it only after you have delivered all of the boxes to their owners.

Until we meet again,
Bronwyn

I glanced around the room looking for a closet door. I have lived here for months, and I have opened every closet in the attic. I opened all of the drapes. I made sure all of the lights were on. I did not see a door anywhere. I walked around the room removing anything on the walls. There was an antique Victorian full length mirror that hung on an inner wall. It was much heavier than I expected. Slowly, I removed it from the wall. The mirror hid a small door.

I reached for the doorknob. It was secure. I inserted the key. Apprehensively, I opened the door. The smell of neglect rose into the air. Everything was as Bronwyn described. My mother's and father's boxes bawled for me to touch them. I chose to search the contents before delivering the boxes.

I opened my mother's box. My heart raced. My palms started sweating. I glanced into the box. The secrets of the historic district floated into the sky. In a rage of terror, I searched for evidence of what my father did to Ms. Sally. Nothing. I searched again. I took the box and emptied its contents onto the floor of the attic. In an incredibly precise manner, I examined every artifact. There were several items that depicted my father's appalling life. There were photos of him taking bribes from state senators and business leaders and photographs of dinners with young women, where he was holding their hands. Ms. Sally and her abuse was not there. I continued searching. Suddenly, I realized that my mother was not mentioned in this box. She was not in any picture or other condemning artifact. I rose frantically from the floor. I reached to my father's box. I took it to a separate space on the floor, away from her box. I dumped its contents. The contents were equal.

I looked in the other boxes. All of the boxes contained the exact same artifacts. Eric's and Emily's affairs were documented, as were their membership in Jackson. Elizabeth's miscarriages and Patrick's addictions were part of the contents. Grace and Sawyer were not traveling around the world; rather, they were visiting their gay son in New York, who had a partner and children. The Harding's affair was photographed extensively, but also his affair with a young male Army ranger. The Winchester's real estate debacle was a repetitive act that began years ago.

It was all there, all of the sins of the historic district.

In that moment, I was proud of myself. I was proud that I opened each of the boxes. My actions did not engender all of the pain that people could have felt had I obeyed my uncle's wishes. I sat in the floor examining the contents of boxes. In that moment, I realized that I was the keeper of the sins of the district. I held the deepest and darkest secrets of my neighbors. I was not sure that my soul was capable of such knowledge.

The doorbell rang. I left the secrets scattered on the floor. I walked down and reached for the doorknob. As I touched it, I became afraid. I glanced through a small hole in the door and saw Auden. He had never visited before. I opened the door. He invited himself into the foyer. In a very frank tone, he asked me to lock the door and follow him to the basement. Without hesitation, I followed. I became nervous, yet I trusted him.

The basement was half the size of the first floor. It was windowless and the fluorescent lights were abrasive. The room was bare other than a small sofa. The white walls were sterile and uninviting. He walked toward the fireplace. Slowly, he reached for the statue on the right side of the mantle. The fireplace opened to reveal a tunnel. He flipped the light switch. All of his movements were purposeful and repetitive. It was obvious that this was not his first time. We walked into the tunnel. There was another door approximately ten feet from the doorway from which we exited. He reached into his pocket and unlocked the door. We walked into another tunnel.

Again, he reached for the light switch, knowing its placement on the wall. We walked for approximately three minutes.

My heart raced. He had not spoken to me since he commanded me to follow him to the basement. He walked briskly and adamantly. He knew where we were going. We reached another door on the left. He opened it with a different key. The lights were already bright. We walked into a medium sized room with mahogany bookshelves and large leather sofas. There was a bar with every liquor that one could enjoy.

Corbin walked over and offered me a bourbon. He was well-mannered tonight. He did not seem himself. He shook my hand with the firm shake that indicated his hunger. The light in the room flickered off the contacts in his eyes, and I noticed something different. I could not identify it, but there was something different about Corbin. Auden sat on a sofa on the left side of the room. He remained silent. They were the only two people I knew. Maxwell Carmichael walked over and introduced himself to me. He was a Judge from Hattiesburg. His wealth was apparent. The Rolex on his right arm was worth north of one hundred thousand. His suit and shoes were also evidence of his social class. Beau Aldridge walked toward me and offered his hand. It was soft and smooth. His face was almost wrinkle free. His short salt and pepper hair was parted perfectly on the left side of his head. His seersucker suit reminded me of old southern values. He lived in Greenville, Mississippi on the west side of the state. He was an older man who was the largest land owner in the southeast. His timber made millions of dollars every year.

Davis Lexington was from Meridian and was a state senator, who never lost an election in twenty years. Brooks Montgomery owned a manufacturing plant that made parts for car makers outside of Oxford. He was also planning to run for governor in the next election. I knew the name. His son went to Ole Miss with me; I am certain that he was in my fraternity. Keaton Rothschild was a real estate developer from Jackson. His wealth was also evident in his appearance and his choice of bourbon. The 27 year old Pappy Van Winkle that he sipped perfectly was a thirty thousand dollar bottle. I was shocked at the men who surrounded me.

After the introductions, Maxwell explained that I was the newest member of the machine. I was replacing Bronwyn who replaced my grandfather, who replaced my great grandfather who was a Mississippi governor. It all made sense. I glanced at Corbin questioningly. Maxwell read my face perfectly. "Corbin replaces his father, Yates Willingham," Maxwell stated.

He explained that the men in this room met only when necessary and in different parts of the state, sometimes the country. We were to never speak of the machine in public, nor were we to speak of the things that we discussed in meetings. There was a procedure to the machine's processes and decisions. Auden was going to serve as my mentor. I was told that I would learn more as time progressed, that tonight was a celebratory night because they have waited years for the machine to become complete again. That night had arrived.

Corbin

AS I WALKED WITH JACKSON THROUGH THE TUNNEL
toward his house, I knew he had questions. I remember when I
was new a few years ago. It all happened so fast. For months, my
mind swam in the murkiness that the machine created. I wanted
to know it all. Auden was a great mentor. He helped me understand, as he would now help Jackson.

When we reached his house, we entered through the mantel.
We walked upstairs and into the parlor. He offered me a bourbon, which I accepted. We sat, and he stared at me with a deep
stare, wanting answers. I was not his mentor, but I thought that
I could share some insight with him. I began to tell him about
our history.

The machine has existed since Mississippi became the
twentieth state. It has been the guiding force that controls the
political and social atmosphere of the state. It began with one
man from each of the wealthiest families in the new state and
has remained within those families. As one member is admit-
ted, he must choose his heir immediately. Being a part of the
machine is a life time commitment. There is no possibility of

224

being released. We were chosen for our positions because of who we are. I continued to explain to Jackson the power of the men.

All of the major events that took place in the state's history can be connected to the machine. We were against the Civil War. Slavery divided the men, but we were able to realize the importance of our power as a group. We helped the first two women get elected to the state legislature. We assisted in the death of two State Supreme Court justices and three governors. We helped choose the first African American Supreme Court Justice. As I was discussing some of the things that we have been involved in, Jackson excused himself and ran upstairs.

He returned with a box. He opened the lid and revealed hundreds of newspaper articles. As I sporadically searched through them, I realized what Bronwyn had done. He had collected newspaper articles for every event that the machine had caused since his membership. Jackson realized the same truth. Bronwyn was a fastidious man, who survived off routines and structure. For him, everything in life must be categorized and placed in its rightful space.

I found the pictures of Jackson during his doctoral graduation. He saw me holding them. We both realized what the photographs revealed beyond the surface representations.

Jackson's face was fastened on the new knowledge. I knew he needed time to process. I needed time when I first entered the group. I walked to the bar and reached for the bourbon. I poured more into his glass. He asked about recent events. I shared with him our involvement in the Winchester's arrest, the fire at Eric's house, and the Jason Cortez case. He realized that it was not by chance that Auden was the defendant's attorney.

We sat and discussed our history for another hour. As I revealed our actions, he realized the power of the machine. The bourbon helped calm him.

Auden

IT WAS NICE TO GATHER WITH THE OTHER MEN LAST
night. We had to discuss my current case and how the machine
was going to intervene. It was also nice to see Bronwyn's replace-
ment. Jackson seemed so unsure when he left us. I am sure that
Corbin gave him some superficial information, but Corbin does
not truly understand us. He is still new to the brotherhood.

The machine has been around since Mississippi's inception.
It commenced with representatives from the eight wealthiest
families in Mississippi. When a person becomes a member, he
must choose which family member will replace him when he
dies. Bronwyn chose Jackson because he did not have a son of
his own, though Jackson was practically his son. They were extremely close. Jackson was a good choice. He was smart, successful, and even tempered.

The machine has controlled state politics for two hundred
and three years. We have influenced nearly half of the guber-
natorial elections in Mississippi and fourteen presidential elections. We have been involved in three governor's deaths and
one presidential death, James Garfield. The eight men in the

machine meet only when necessary and a majority vote is necessary for us to intervene.

The only event in which we were not able to intervene was the election of Jefferson Davis as the President of the Confederate States. The machine was divided four against four. They met and postulated their opinions for three days, but no one was willing to change his vote. They were divided on seceding from the Union and on Jefferson's abilities to lead the confederacy.

I know that Jackson will be okay. He simply needs time to adjust to his new position in the organization and the community.

Abby

JACKSON SHOULD GET THE LETTER TODAY. IT WAS MY decision. I can't tell him. He doesn't need to know. When I was done there, I began the long drive to Charleston. I notified the bank that I had a family medical emergency. I have been with the bank for nearly 15 years; they understood and approved my leave of absence. I am not going back to Culpepper. The woman called my name into the open air. I stood. I was sure. I walked through the door and down the long hallway to another smaller room. I took my position. Another woman came into the room and touched my shoulder. It was her way of comforting me. But, I was sure. She handed me a pamphlet with all of the information that I would need over the coming days. We spoke in quiet and solemn tones, an almost whispering voice. She asked if I had questions. I did not. She reached into the pocket of her white coat and produced the pill. She handed me a small glass of water. I placed the pill into my mouth. Slowly, I raised the glass to my lips. The lukewarm water was adequate. I swallowed more water. There did not seem to be enough water. I needed more. I returned to my car. The tears began falling before I could start the car. I began the long drive to Charleston.

Jackson

I WOKE AROUND NOON WITH THE THIRD HANGOVER of my life and by far the most painful one. I also woke to find a letter from Abby in the mailbox. She had returned to Charleston. She did not want to see me because the pain of her leaving would be too difficult for her. She wrote a stunningly beautiful letter explaining why we could not be together. I was angry. I deserved to speak to her. She made a decision about us and excluded me from it. She would not answer my calls nor my texts. She was a coward.

I needed to purge the toxins from my body. I ran south to the end of Magnolia, and through the park, past the confederate statue, toward the river walk. I needed to sweat and to reflect on last night and this morning. My soul needed the release.

I ran harder than I have in a long time. I was focused. I was angry. I was unsure. There were pictures of me at my graduation. Does that mean that I am not worthy of my degree? What did the machine do to guarantee my graduation? Why was Abby really leaving? Were they the cause of that too? The questions inundated my mind. The questions caused me to run faster. I just wanted to escape them. I wanted my old life back. I wanted Virginia and my old wooden desk. I missed the smell of old books and long hours teaching students to love Faulkner.

I ran until I found myself in the backyard of my parents' home. I stopped and fell into the old iron swing that rested there. My sweat dripping through the holes in the metal seat. The memories broke me. This place broke me. I was tired of carrying the sins of my father for all of these years. I was tired of the pain that he caused Ms. Sally. I was tired of knowing that he hated Blake and caused him so much harm. The year of living in this neighborhood broke me. I thought that I could do it. I thought that I was strong enough. And now, it broke Abby. I lost one of the most beautiful people I have ever met. It broke us.

I shattered into the grass. The front of the swing tapping my shoulders and the back of my neck as it swayed back and forth from my fall out of it. I fell into the grass and cried. I simply could not exist in my former self any longer. For years, I simply existed, lost in the guilt of someone else's sins. They broke me into millions of pieces. I lay in the grass crying, shattered and crying.

Ms. Sally

"JACKY, WHAT'S WRONG WITH YOU? WHY ARE YOU OUT here crying?"

"Ms. Sally, I am so sorry. I didn't tell anyone. I am so sorry. There is no excuse. I am so sorry."

I sat beside Jackson in the swing. He felt like a wet wash rag in my arms. Crying and carrying on.

"Jacky, you listen here. Stop that crying. You are not a baby. Hush it up."

"Ms. Sally, I was so scared. I was scared."

"Honey, I knew you were. I was too. I lived in that house now 30 years. I had insurance all of those years. I got a car to piddle around in. I got to raise four good kids. If you or I told anyone, I would have been kicked out. I would have lost it all. It was worth it two maybe three times every few months of that old bastard touching me. Most of the time he'd be drunk from the whiskey."

"Ms. Sally, It wasn't worth it. It could not have been worth it."

"I'm going tell you something. You can't ever tell a soul. Just like you didn't tell anyone about what he did. You hold what I am going to tell you deep in your heart. Understand?"

232

"Yes, Ma'am."

"I'm serious boy. Never a soul."

"Yes, Ma'am."

"When your mother passed, everyone stopped visiting your daddy. Sarah Beth has not been in that house since before your mother passed. So, when your father got cancer, it moved so fast, he wanted to die at home, so I agreed to take care of him. Remember? He got real sick in June of that year. Your uncle went to Europe with that Boyce man for a month. Sarah Beth wasn't coming by. You were in Virginia. And, Blake, he was off playing pro ball. The doctor put that tube in his throat and he came home to die. They thought it would be a week or so.

The nurse, Nikki, was my best friend's daughter. Nikki came out to the house every morning at ten to check on your daddy. I'd tell Nikki that if anything happened I would give her a ring. So Nikki would leave after she did her check. I paid attention to how much medicine was in the bag after the first night. When Nikki left the next morning I walked in that room, and I turned that clip at his arm to stop the morphine from going in him. Just like I saw her do. Then, I took the littlest sewing needle I could find. I poked a hole by the seam of the bag on the right side. I let that morphine run through that hole into a tall glass. I set that glass on the table by that bastard's bed. He could see it, but it was out of reach for him.

He was in terrible pain all day and all night. Then at 8 in the morning I walked in and turned that clip at his arm again. The rest of the medicine below the hole that I made flowed in him. The morphine knocked his ass out. Nikki would come in and check on him. He'd be out cold. This happened every day for three weeks. They thought he was just a mean old man not ready to give up the fight. I guess when the Good Lord said he suffered enough, he took him. But, that bastard didn't deserve grace to die by. He didn't deserved it. So, Jacky you stop that crying. Dry your eyes. We are going to be okay. Now, get up, give me your hand. We are going in that house."

Jackson

I STOOD WITH HER AND WE WALKED FROM THE IRON swing to the back veranda. I opened the door, and together we walked into the sunroom. My parents had this room added to the house when I was in high school. It was my favorite room in the house. In the spring, I would open the windows and listen to the rain until the melodic sound would drown me into a nap. I loved napping in that room.

We walked into the kitchen and the memories of cooking with my mother bombarded me. I stood silently, remembering standing in this exact space when I told the second most important person in my life that I saw what that monster did to her. It was here nearly fifteen years ago that I shared my guilt and my sin with her.

My eyes watered.

I walked into the hallway, the oil painting depicting him was still hanging on the wall. His condescension was palpable. I walked into every room and endured the good and evil memories as each room emancipated them from me.

Ms. Sally and I walked into the foyer and stared at the long ornate staircase. It was the same staircase that Blake attempted to skateboard down and broke his leg. It was the same staircase that we all rode the banisters as if they were ocean waves returning us to the shore. I climbed the structure seeking penance for my sins. When we reached the top, we turned right and walked down the hallway to my parents' bedroom. This time the door seemed much harder to push open than when I was a young boy seeking peace from a bad dream.

I opened the door as if I was entering Grendel's lair. The room remained the same as it did when he slept here.

We walked over. Anger consumed me. I tore the bedding from the bed. I threw his pictures from the night stands, causing the glass to break on the hardwood floors. I threw the mattress against the wall. I tore the drapes from the windows. The rods clamoring to the floor. His clothing flew from the closets and dressers. The anger changed to anguish. I dropped to my knees and wept. The tears escaped my soul too rapidly to speak or to catch a full breath. I kneeled on the floor as if I was praying, praying without words, only the tears praying.

Ms. Sally kneeled with me. She held me. The woman whose pain far exceeded my pain held me and allowed my pain to fall upon her. She held me for an hour. She prayed for me, as only a faithful mother can do. As we sat there, each tear released my guilt.

Sarah Beth

I STOOD ON THE PORCH AS THE MOVERS REMOVED
every remembrance of Preston W. Kensington III from our
family home. I watched as his oil portrait disappeared into the
moving truck. I saw boxes of his personal items stacked on the
side wall of the truck ready to be driven away forever.

I walked around the house and found Jackson in the backyard. Several years ago, our parents decided to build a stone fireplace in the backyard. It became a gathering place for neighborhood parties and family gatherings. The fireplace was at least
three times the size of a normal fireplace within a home. It was
a beautiful addition to the gardens. The fireplace was the focal
point of their new backyard arrangement. Our mother commissioned custom seating and dining to accent the area.

Jackson had started the fire. The rolling red and blue colors
of the fire proved its strength. There were several boxes of Preston's things situated around the fireplace. Jackson held a bottle
of Woodford and two Waterford glasses. He offered me one
glass and began pouring the bourbon into the circular container.
He continued pouring into his own glass. We toasted the loss

and destruction of the monster and vowed that he would have no more control in our lives. After the toast, Jackson chose a picture of Preston and tossed it into the fire. He glanced around and chose a Burberry dress shirt, which he tossed it into the fire.

I reached for a photograph of me and Preston in the backyard swing. I walked to the fireplace. I sipped my bourbon. As I viewed the photo, I remembered that day. I was a teenager who had just won my first state title in soccer. I sat on the hearth. The stone was hard, but at this moment it was also comforting. I placed the photo at the edge of the fire. The blue flames began to destroy the image of the man who hurt so many people. I pushed the photo completely into the purifier.

For several hours, we burned the monster into the air. The pain and the anguish that he caused us and others floated into the universe, dismantled and deconstructed. His power and our guilt released forever into the heavens.

Jackson

SARAH BETH RETURNED TO HER FAMILY. THE FIRE was diminishing. I walked to the mailbox. A letter from Ole Miss was there. Cautiously, I opened it as I walked toward the backyard. I glanced upward and saw Ms. Sally walk into the cottage. I paused in front of the old iron swing. My laptop rested on the right of the metal seat. I read the letter aloud.

> *Dr. Kensington, It is with great pleasure that I welcome you to The University of Mississippi as a tenured full professor in the English Department. The department, the college, and the broader university will benefit from having you join our faculty. I have included your offer letter and other documents for you to sign and return to my office. We are excited that you will become part of the Ole Miss family. Welcome home!*

I folded the letter and returned it to the envelope. I knew that they had something to do with this. I had not applied to Ole Miss, but I held an offer letter from the university president. The machine wanted me here.

I also knew that she left because of them.

It was time for me to return home.

I sat in the iron swing of my family home as the evening sun set quietly in the distance. The purging of my home was the beginning of the remedy for my soul. The calmness of an early summer evening surrounded me. The Purple Martins darted through the sky, devouring the mosquitoes. My laptop rested easily on my lap. My fingers began to furiously strike the keys. The words flowing from my soul, jumping into the air and landing precisely on the screen. The black letters revealing the story of a neighborhood entrenched in the mangled secrets of humanity. The enigmatic lives of a group of people living in the Deep South, people who cared more about appearances than the truth or each other. It is a story of love, of hatred, of secrets, and of grace. It is *Magnolia Avenue.*

9 781950 794287